Wish

AN ENCHANTED ARDOR STORY

JODI KENDRICK

SOULGATE PUBLISHING

Dragon Island
Dragon Heat

Enchanted Ardor
Wish

EveL Worlds : FUCN'A

Tough Nut
Diamond in the Ruff
Honeyed Nut
Gorilla in the Hiss
FUCN'A Collection One
Pedigree Collection

Finely Aged
Dragon Steel

Global Paranormal Security Agency

Awakened
Surfacing
Polestar
Aquatic Investigations
Prowler

The Kindred Chronicles

Healer
Mercenary

The Soaring Dragon Chronicles

Return Flight
Changeling

Chapter One

The ornate door swung open, revealing an opulent foyer for Gena to step through. Her spiked heels announced her arrival on the glossy marble floor as a butler stepped forward to relieve her of her coat. She relinquished it happily, hating heavy winter coats and the need for them in general. She preferred the warmer, dryer weather she spent her early life basking in.

All the same, she made her way through the lush, glittering white and silver festive décor, following a new servant toward the faint music and low chatter.

Drawing a deep breath, she entered the large room, eyes scanning for the hostess, Quinn O'Clery.

The tiny box in her hand, although almost weightless, felt anything but. She was trusting Olivia Boncoeur on this.

Djinn wishes were rare.

Unconditional wishes legendarily rare.

Olivia had requested this special gift for her long-time friend, and Gena couldn't find it in herself to refuse.

A loner by nature and habit, hating parties and crowds, here she was, attending as a proxy.

A graceful blonde stepped forward with a warm smile.

Gena set her shoulders and returned the brilliant smile, guessing this was the legendary woman herself, Quinn O'Clery.

"Welcome, Gena, I was sorry to hear Olivia couldn't make it, but I'm delighted you're here in her place. Would you like a drink?"

"Thank you, no. I don't plan to stay. I just wanted to ensure that I delivered Olivia's gift, hand to hand." She smiled again, trying to let her nerves slide away as she glanced at all the strange faces around the room. Her gaze snagged on one in particular, assessed, and then continued on before coming back.

Turning her eyes back to Quinn, she held up the small box.

Quinn had been watching Gena closely, and a knowing smile quirked the corner of her mouth when she laid her hand over Gena's. "Please join me for a drink, and maybe a bite to eat. Besides, that fabulous red dress you're wearing would go to waste. Is it a *Wong*? A dress like that needs to be flaunted."

"Alright. One drink."

"Perfect." Quinn winked at her, and she relaxed.

"Please," she said, holding the box up to Quinn again. "Olivia's gift."

Quinn's expression turned curious as she accepted the little box. "What is it?"

"Open it," Gena prompted.

With a last glance at Gena, Quinn lifted the lid. A tiny ornament was nestled on red satin. On its face was etched the image of a pair of elegant eyes peering through a curling flame. She raised a querying brow. "It's lovely."

"This is an unconditional wish. Whatever your heart desires. Use it wisely."

Quinn's perfectly curated brows rose. "This is incredibly generous," she said, her voice breathless.

"Olivia said you were special and she wanted to gift you something worthy of your own generosity."

"Thank you, Gena."

Gena could see that Quinn clearly understood the significance of such a special gift and she relaxed a little, sensing that the wish would be used with careful consideration.

"Drink?" Quinn prompted again.

Gena nodded. "Please."

"This way," Quinn led Gena further into the room, closer to the unknown faces, including the handsome one she'd spied earlier. Her heart beat faster the further into the room she walked.

Bayn's attention turned toward the newcomer in the red dress, talking to Quinn by the entrance to the ball room.

Her presence called to him like no treasure hoard ever had.

He needed to get closer.

As soon as the conversation around him turned, he excused himself from his companions and drifted toward where Quinn had led her guest for a drink.

With a glance at Bayn, Quinn picked up a second glass and held it out for him as he approached, switching it with his empty one.

He smiled in thanks, then turned his attention to the beautiful stranger.

"Bai Yun Long, this is Gena Black. She's only here for a drink then has to jet. But I'm confident you can persuade her to stay a little longer." She placed a warm hand on each of their upper arms.

"I'll do my best," he said, sparing Quinn a respectful grin.

She winked at him, gave them a little pat and moved away to greet the next guest.

"Everyone calls me Bayn. Have we met?" He asked immediately. "I'm sure we have."

Gena's bemused smile made him chuckle.

"I know, not very original opening line, is it? But really, have we?"

"In a way, yes," she said, cryptic.

This wouldn't do, but she seemed reluctant to reveal their past encounter.

"That long ago, huh?" he raised his glass. "Alright then. New beginning?"

She searched his face for a long moment. A sense of unease roiled up through his gut, displacing some of the party cheer. But then she smiled, lifting her glass. "To new beginnings."

The unease disappeared in a snap.

They touched rims with a soft clink, the sound of it reverberating through him like one of the angel bells affixed to the nearby Christmas tree that dominated the room.

How could he not clearly recall this beauty, despite how drawn he was to her?

He tamped down the rising desire to possess.

He was a new man and was learning to control his baser, instinctive urges in this modern day and age.

Bayn no longer swooped in and claimed whatever he wanted. Well, not quite in the same way.

His gaze swept the length of her tailor-fit red dress. Exquisite.

"Do you intend to tell me where we've met before?"

Her dark eyes considered him for a few seconds and took on a mischievous glint. "Not quite yet."

"Quinn has a lovely courtyard," he prompted, raising his forearm as an offering.

Sliding an elegant hand over it, she followed him through the wonderland toward the open French doors. He stopped briefly along the way, introducing her to other guests as they went.

The outdoor decor of the courtyard was an extension of the interior winter-land enchantment, with cooler, crisper air.

Outside, nearly alone, Bayn had a better sense of her magic. She was as ancient as himself. Their previous encounter could have been centuries ago.

But Bayn's memory was exceptional. He didn't forget faces.

His familiarity of her was on a different level.

She wasn't dragon like himself.

Was she a shifter? Perhaps he'd only seen her in animal form.

No, her magic scent was different.

He decided to go back to basics and start from the beginning again. "Tell me, how did you meet Quinn?"

"I met her at the entrance to the ballroom."

He raised a brow at that. "You didn't know her before this evening?"

She shook her head. "I'm here as a favor to a dear mutual friend, Olivia Boncoeur."

"Oh, I see." His second brow rose to join the first. Bayn knew Olivia, though he hadn't seen her in centuries. Not since...well, not since an incident a very long time ago. Best forgotten. "Alright then, tell me something of yourself."

"How about you go first," she countered.

Chapter Two

B efore Gena realized the time, the evening had flown in a whirl of silvery white and crystal. And in Bayn's blinding smile and twinkling dark eyes.

The sounds of party merriment and the scent tones of the other beings mingled with the bouquets of hundreds of white roses.

Gena had never attended such an event in all her centuries. It was incredible. She'd been part of them countless times but never enjoyed the privilege as an attendee. Usually just as some token ornament, on occasion as a center piece.

She'd managed to go the entire evening without revealing the past connection between herself and Bayn.

She wasn't yet ready to face their past relationship—one that he did not recognize, as it was. And she could sense the change in him over the intermittent years.

His desire to possess her in those early moments was overwhelmingly powerful, and the ensuing self-control remarkable for one of his nature.

This piqued her curiosity.

Her attraction to him was unmistakable.

She'd always been drawn to him, but their earlier circumstances were not conducive to the kind of relationship she craved. Infatuated, observing him from afar. Longing for his companionship. The beauty and power of his glittering beast.

She'd been there, for so long. But he'd never seen her. Not the 'real' Gena. Just another shiny object in his impressive, extensive hoard. Never the living, feeling being that she actually was.

But now, stripped of her past as she was, and unblinded by his, maybe—just maybe—they could truly see each other. For at least an evening.

Bayn had been busy in the last centuries building a new life.

Those nearly forgotten feelings of fascination rose up, overwhelming. But her new self-awareness found the control to balance the need to give.

All evening, Gena took. She took his company. She took his stories and insights, and in turn hoarded these bits of information close to her heart. She would take each one out to inspect later when she was home alone and could think. For now, she gave in to the party atmosphere she'd initially resisted.

Gena gave nothing back to Bayn.

When she finally decided to take her leave, and they parted ways, she'd still not volunteered anything of herself.

He hadn't made the connection.

And she was okay with that. In fact, she was secretly enjoying the mystery game.

But would he lose interest once he solved it?

Now, he walked her back to where she'd stepped into his life again, to say her good-byes to Quinn and give her thanks for such an enchanting evening.

In the foyer, the butler held her coat for her.

As she reached for it, Bayn caught her hand and pulled it to his lips, eyes on hers.

Her mind conjured images of his lips touching hers and drifting to other places as those intense eyes held hers just as they did now.

His magic flared against hers in that instant, as though he sensed her thoughts.

She couldn't know if he really did, but his sensual mouth turned up at the corner, transforming the handsome angular face with boyish charm. He still dazzled her. Even after all this time.

She drew in a deep breath to steady the onslaught of emotional and carnal thoughts ravaging her mind.

"Goodnight, Bayn."

"We'll meet again?"

"Perhaps." She glanced down at the coat the butler still held for her, but left it where it was.

Her heels clicked on the last few steps of the marble as she passed through the doorway into the wintry night air.

She was no longer the complete prisoner of a golden lamp, lost among the hoard of other beautiful shiny gold treasures.

With a snap of her fingers, she dissipated in a black swirling mist she knew would leave tiny traces of her magic behind.

Bayn stared at the dissipating black mist.

He spared the butler a glance, who in turn regarded him with a bemused stare, still holding the abandoned coat.

Bayn reached for it. "May I? I can return it to Ms. Black."

"I'm not sure she particularly cared for it, sir," the butler said.

"All the same," he said, as the butler handed the garment to him.

The surge caused by the use of her magic triggered a memory. A certain frequency—a tenor that he recognized. The undertone that had drawn him in the first place.

Images of his lost hoard—a cascade of gold and glittering gems in the vault of his den, so long ago.

Before Olivia Boncoeur changed his life.

That tang of magic had been attached to a particular object. A beautiful one he'd owned, among thousands.

A rare treasure that simply occupied space among the coins and jewels and other gilded things.

He had no need for magical items. He was magical himself.

A hint of shame needled itself into his consciousness when he thought of his beloved hoard, and Olivia Boncoeur.

He straightened his spine.

That was the old dragon.

He was a new dragon now.

Hoards were long in his past. He did things differently.

But the taste of her magic and the memory of that object of his desire mingled in his mind. What was it?

The image of a golden lamp floated to the forefront of his memory.

No.

It couldn't be. Could it?

Was it possible?

A djinn as ancient as the earth imprisoned in that golden lamp, forgotten in his hoard.

She should have been cherished, but she'd been a prisoner.

And now she wasn't.

He stared at the empty space outside the still-open door. Olivia Boncoeur must have freed her. Who else would have been so selfless? He surely hadn't been.

Bayn had to find her.

Not to possess her as he once obliviously had.

But to know her.

That encounter with Olivia Bonceur had changed his life forever. And apparently was still changing it, centuries later.

Gena had simply disappeared in a cloud of glittering onyx mist. Where was she now?

He glanced down at the coat in his hand and smiled.

To the butler he said, "Please tell your mistress I will contact her in the morning." Then he stepped out into the night air and in turn, shifted into a mass of crystal mist, the coat absorbed along with him, and rose into the sky.

Chapter Three

Gena was in her dining room reviewing her bills.

The joys of living a mortal life.

But still, she was free and that was what mainly mattered.

After the party, she'd gone to check in with Olivia, of course, to confirm that she had indeed delivered the gift as requested. And yes, she had indeed socialized. And yes, yes, she had spent the evening talking to someone. A very handsome someone.

However, she gave the identity of the gentleman in question with great reluctance.

"And he had no idea who you were?" Olivia had exclaimed with a snort of disgust that Bayn had had no clue to her identity.

Gena didn't mind.

"It was fun. I got to play at being a mystery woman for a few hours. No harm done. Some nice conversation at an elegant mansion," she shrugged, "A great night out. Thanks to you." She added for good measure.

Olivia scowled. "Who'd have thought you'd have an enraptured evening with Bayn Long."

"Olivia, really, so what if he didn't know I existed all those years ago? It wasn't the end of the world."

Grumbling followed. "So, what you're saying is that you liked him?"

Gena shrugged.

Olivia blew out an exasperated breath.

"What's the matter darling?" Nick asked, as he shuffled into the warm kitchen for another cup of coffee, and planted a whiskery kiss on his wife's cheek.

"Nothing's wrong. Gena met a man."

"Nice, good for you for getting out." He winked and sauntered off again.

"What are the odds?" Olivia said, once he was gone.

"I don't know, but it's pretty incredible."

Olivia threw her another thoughtful look. "And you still feel the same way about him? After all this time?"

Gena looked down into her cup.

"Awe, honey."

"I know you don't understand. And no, it's nothing like Stockholm Syndrome. He really didn't know I existed, it's a whole other thing entirely."

"I don't know about that."

Gena straightened her spine. "It's not the same. Now how about we talk about the schedule, instead? That's the reason you said you couldn't make it to the party yourself in the first place."

Olivia flushed and looked away sipping from her own coffee cup. "Yes, well..."

"Well what? Do you still need help in the shop or not?"

"Maybe a little. Nick's always running behind, but he's been particularly distracted this year. The crew are struggling to keep up with the orders."

Gena blew out a breath, "Okay, I'll check in and see what I can do.

"Thanks, love."

Gena smiled at her best friend. "Anything for you, you know that."

"Right, so you've made contact?" Bayn grunted into his cell.

"Invitation sent, you just have to practice your patience and wait, and see if she takes you up on it."

"And you've got the right address?"

"Yes, Bayn, I have the right address. I know what I'm doing. This is why you came to me, right?"

"Right."

"Bayn, are you nervous? I've never known you to be so insistent before."

"No," he said quickly. "Lots of work on my plate, which reminds me, I should get back to it."

"Uh huh." Quinn's voice on the other end of the line was skeptical. "I'll call you as soon as she reaches out."

"Thanks."

Quinn disconnected the call and Bayn sat at his desk, staring at the far wall.

Then he scowled hard. He didn't get nervous. And he wasn't insistent. He was just following up, like he always did.

Persistent.

It was different.

He glanced at the long list of emails jamming up his inbox and turned away from them toward the skyline visible outside his floor to ceiling office windows. These days he was working and living in Toronto. The city lights were just beginning to wink on. With a glance to his left, he waited moments for the sky to darken just a shade or two more before the CN Tower lit up, casting a colorful glow into his office. The streets far below were alive, and he could see ships sliding across the surface of Lake Ontario.

Distracted for the moment, his thoughts immediately returned to Gena.

Bayn had seldom been surprised in his long, long lifetime, but since the night of the party he'd been trying to wrap his mind around the fact that he'd just met the most intriguing woman of his life, and that she'd actually spent decades, if not centuries, trapped in his vault. And he'd been ignorant of the situation.

The ridiculousness of it.

He thought back to what his life was like at that time. He was different now.

Then, he collected and hoarded, as per his nature to do so. Existing in a world of shiny gold brilliance, not bothering with the world at large, unless it was to find a cow to eat, or something shiny to break the monotony of dragon life.

Now, since Olivia had tilted his world view, he'd become part of it. But not completely.

He still lived alone.

Dragons were mostly solitary creatures. But in the last while, he had to acknowledge that he was becoming broody and no longer content with the single man status.

He wanted more, but hadn't been able to put a claw on what it was he wanted.

Until Gena walked through Quinn's door.

And that had been months ago, now.

Warmer weather had come after the holidays; the St. Lawrence River had cracked open, letting the ocean-going ships into the heartland of the lakes district. And it seemed his heart had also cracked open, longing for something more.

But not just anyone.

He had to admit, really, that Gena had been the one to create that first tiny fissure. Then time and loneliness had begun to set it.

He wanted to see her again.

So, he'd caved and called Quinn.

He'd never asked Quinn for a set up before, but extreme times called for extreme measures.

Not to mention, he'd been unable to track Gena himself. Seems she kept herself very low under the social radar.

And as for Olivia. Well, he wasn't going to go that route. They had their differences, and he sincerely doubted she'd be the one to help him out.

He watched as a red and white cargo ship eased into port. A Canadian liner come home.

Maybe Gena wouldn't be the one. Maybe she wasn't his mate.

He thought she might be.

But he was old enough to know that sometimes life threw a hard turn and sent you sailing in a new direction.

Still, he knew, deep down, that Gena was the next step.

Chapter Four

"Yes, Olivia. No, I won't. Don't worry.. . Olivia, it's coffee."

Gena rolled her eyes.

In the intervening months, she'd done her best to help her friend really understand. She knew that the reason Olivia didn't, initially, was because Gena hadn't talked much about her life in the lamp. What was there to say?

Long tedious hours, alone, sitting around with little to do. While she couldn't leave the lamp, she could sort-of spy outside of it.

She glanced at it on her mantel piece.

Yes, she kept it. She didn't know why. Okay, that wasn't entirely true.

It had been a gift from her father.

And, she kept it because she was afraid someone else would get their hands on it and figure out how to put her back in it. That, and she wasn't sure how to live without it yet.

So why wasn't it securely locked away?

She shrugged at herself.

No one ever came over. She was still alone. No one could ever get into her place, either. She used a key to lock it, but it was also warded against intruders.

This self-imprisonment was safe. And self-imposed. Her decision.

She'd been content living these last few centuries as she was. Making her own choices, going out when and wherever she wanted to go.

Even if, in the early days, that meant dealing with thugs and predators.

She could take care of herself.

She still had her magic.

But she kept it in check. Without the curse locking her in place, she had no idea if it was finite or not, so she used it sparingly.

She ended her call with Olivia and picked up the invitation.

It was a simple coffee date.

She thought he'd forgotten about her.

Apparently, months later, he hadn't.

She smiled.

Her memories of him had dimmed over time, but now, since that last run-in at Quinn's party, they replayed through her mind like the movies she'd grown to love. Fully alive, now in color and with incredible soundtracks. The sound track to her memory of that night had been the musical undertone and voices of the other attendees.

But mostly, she remembered the sound of his voice.

Low. Silky. Smooth so that it slid up her spine and tickled her nape when he spoke. Now and then, he'd leaned closer and it coiled in her ear, making her shiver.

She longed for that proximity again.

Nervous excitement curled in her belly as her fingers slid over the thick embossed paper.

Coffee.

She needed a dress. Or new jeans. She had to shop.

No! Coffee. Don't go crazy.

Never mind. Surely there was something appropriate in her closet.

If they made it to another date, then she could shop.

She swallowed the excess energy and resisted the urge to teleport herself to where ever he was and observe. That sort of behavior was no longer acceptable in this day and age.

Reel it in, woman!

Deep breath.

Coffee. Start with that.

She was going crazy inside.

After several more moments, she picked up her phone and dialed.

"Hi Quinn. So nice to hear from you again. Coffee? Let me check my schedule. Hmm, I think I can squeeze that in. 2pm? That sounds doable."

She hung up the phone.

Confirmed.

Now she had to decide if she was going to teleport to her coffee date or travel like a normal person.

But it would be an awful long trip from Ottawa to Toronto for a coffee date.

Details. She could work that out later.

She was going for coffee with Bayn.

She had to find the right clothes for this. With a glance, she considered her wardrobe.

Maybe just a little bit of shopping would be okay. It was a lovely evening out and everything, and the walk to the mall wasn't far.

She snatched her favorite purse from the hook by the door and slid her feet into her shoes.

Shopping it was.

Bayn sat at the cafe table like he was casually observing the crowd, bored, killing time between meetings.

It took a lot of effort to ease the tension in his posture to his normal state.

Drawing his phone from his jacket pocket, he glanced at the time then quickly scrolled through messages and emails to take his mind off the wait.

Two minutes till she was due to arrive.

He was mentally resigning himself to the potential likelihood that she might not show. But then reminded himself that no one ever bailed on one of Quinn's invitations.

He drew a deep breath and let it seep out through his parted lips.

By now he'd stopped looking up every time the door opened, but was well aware that it had.

A gust of cool spring air breezed through the coffee shop carrying her scent with it.

She'd come.

He glanced up as she slid between other small tables and stopped before him.

He stood to greet her, smiling at the pinkened tip of her nose. The air was still crisp, despite the warming days.

"Hello."

"Hello," he responded. "Coffee?" he added, like the awkward young men he'd observed over the years.

She smiled, "of course. To go? I'd love to see your city."

Perfect.

Orders in hand, he guided her out and along the busy evening streets of downtown Toronto.

Small talk ensued until they found themselves wandering the more crowded, tourist heavy areas where strolling was more of a challenge.

Cups spent, they dropped them into nearby receptacles and turned down a path leading through a small park.

The silence lengthened.

Small talk run out, there were only more personal things to discuss.

"You're one of the shyest people I've ever met," he said, ending the silence.

She glanced at him, startled. She didn't respond.

But he looked into her open face.

She was incredibly lovely.

She'd spent so very long trapped in a cage like a beautiful song bird.

He sighed.

How did one broach such a subject? It was incredibly awkward.

"Olivia Boncoeur freed you." He was sure of it.

"Just after we left your lair."

Her hands twisted in front of her and he placed his over hers.

"Do you want to come to my place for a while, where we can really talk?"

She searched his face, considering, then nodded.

Once inside, she eased out of her coat, "I'll be glad of summer."

He smiled, "Me too."

Settled on his sofa facing one another, the awkwardness stretched between them.

Dragon.

Djinn.

Both at a loss of words.

Bayn was sure he felt something during the magic of the party at Quinn's. Had she felt it too?

Or was that all it really was? Just magic?

He reached out a hand, grasping hers. "Listen, about the past."

A second later, her hand came up and she placed a gentle finger on his lips.

"That's all it is. The past."

Chapter Five

Impulsive.

Gena placed her finger over Bayn's lips to still further questions or talk about the past. She wasn't ready to talk about it yet. He was clearly uncomfortable about some part of it, but she didn't want the words to create a new barrier between them.

She wanted to just be in the moment and learn about each other as they were in this time and place. Not centuries ago.

She wasn't the same being then as she was now. And it was clear to her, neither was he.

"Tell me what you do these days. Clearly you're living as a human, and from the looks of it, very successfully." Her eyes remained on his face. He'd been spectacular in his dragon form. His human shape was so damned hot, she struggled to keep her gaze in check. Her eyes seemed to be constantly drawn back to his handsome face.

His lips left a kiss on her fingertip, which she instantly snatched away from him, sorry for not letting it linger on the fullness of them.

He smiled a lazy smile as he studied her face in turn.

Her heart beat a little faster. Dear Goddess she wanted to climb into his lap right then.

She swallowed, settled back into her corner of the sofa, and folded her hands on her lap. She dropped her gaze from the mischievous glint in his eyes to the shadow of his throat just below his jaw line, then down to the open collar of his button-down shirt, where she wanted to plant a kiss of her own.

Her eyes shot back up to his.

His grin widened as though he could read her thoughts.

"You're an open book, you know."

Heat stung her cheeks and she looked away again.

He leaned forward, fingers sliding over her folded hands. "I like it. I like that about you."

Her gaze shot back to his face, where the grin eased into a sincere smile.

"You are incredibly beautiful."

She blinked at the unexpected compliment. She didn't think it was possible for her to blush any harder, but at this point her cheeks seared with the heat of his words. Her heart pounded harder in her chest.

She lifted her eyes to his and held his gaze.

"That's better," he said, "Too lovely to hide away," he added on a whisper.

This was too much.

Flustered and overwhelmed by his intense, but very much wanted, attention, she blurted, "What do you do for a living?"

His eyes crinkled in the corners but he eased back into his own corner of the sofa.

"Antiques."

A light laugh escaped her. "That's fitting."

He smiled back. "Decided I should do something with what I'd collected over the years."

She finally allowed herself to look around the place more fully, from where they were seated. His townhouse was decorated in a minimalistic yet comfortable tone. Very modern. There wasn't a hint of gold-encrusted jeweled anything, at least not within her view. That didn't mean there wasn't a bedroom stuffed to the ceiling with brilliant treasure.

"No, I'm not hiding what I have left in another room."

She laughed. Busted.

But she did wonder what had happened to it all.

"I returned some of it to where it belonged," he said. "The rest, I sold over the years to Kings and Queens and other rulers that could afford it and bought land in their realms. In more modern times I converted much of it to more real-estate and stock. Now and then, artifacts are sold or donated to museums. Or I trade them for other types of art."

Her eyes drifted to the painting above them. She couldn't see it clearly from her angle, as it was meant to be viewed from further away. But the colors were soft blues, white tones, some gray, and other cool tones. It reminded her of the sky—and the shimmer of his opalescent scales.

She thought of him in his dragon form again. An air dragon, if she recalled correctly.

"Do you spend much time in your natural form?"

He shook his head, "Not as much as I'd like."

"I prefer my human form," she said, "I like the corporeal weight of being attached to the earth. The ability to use human senses." She slid her hand over the fabric covering the arm of the sofa. Her nostrils flared slightly, inhaling the scent of his essence mingled with his cologne. Her eyes drank him in again.

"So do I," he said, voice gone husky.

Her mouth went dry at the intensity of his gaze as he leaned forward.

Her lips parted as she tried to form words, to keep the conversation going, but her brain couldn't function through the rising haze of desire at his proximity.

This...this human sense had never been so strong before.

She'd experienced desire, even indulged herself over the years when the fancy struck her.

But this was different. Every particle in her being was attracted to his, like coal dust on white satin.

A sudden flare of ice blue in his human black eyes drew her attention as his magic surged. Her own responded in kind, a filament reaching out toward the spark.

Her nipples tightened against the fabric of her bra and a tingle of heat in her panties told her what her body wanted next.

"How do you spend your time?" he asked her, now letting his eyes roam over the rest of her body before sweeping back up to her face.

She'd felt it. She'd felt every part of her body respond to wherever his gaze had landed, just as though his hands had been on those places.

"Uhm..." She swallowed the thickening in her throat. "Research. I research properties and artifacts. Sometimes people and events. It depends on what the client's needs are."

"Client's needs." He murmured.

She had her own needs right then, that had nothing to do with research. The tip of her tongue moistened her lips.

"I have a proposition for you."

Yes please!

"I have a project starting next week. Maybe you'd be interested in working on it with me."

... working him... Wait—

Project. Right. *That* kind of work.

Her rising temperature began to descend and logical thought broke through the surface of her rising desire.

"That sounds good." She managed through her tight throat, drawing in a steady deep breath.

"Fantastic. I'll have my assistant email you to schedule something."

She was cooling fast, despite the lingering of his eyes on her face. She held on to that.

"I should go. Early start tomorrow."

Disappointment crossed his face, but he cleared it quickly. "Of course."

She didn't want to go. But this was supposed to be a coffee meet, and the coffee was long gone.

She stood, feeling awkward, extending her hand. "It was lovely catching up with you again."

He stared at her hand, his bemused smile returning as he grasped it between his warm palms, caressing her fingers as he stepped closer to her. "Shall I walk you to your car?"

"No need, I didn't travel by car."

He leaned in.

She instinctively turned her face toward his.

Bayn bypassed her mouth and pressed his warm lips to her cheek, letting the tip of his nose sweep the sensitive spot near her ear.

She shivered.

As he drew back, she said "I would never have suspected you were such a gentleman, Bayn."

He followed her to his door and stepped out onto the porch with her. "I nearly forgot." He stepped back into his house and returned holding a coat.

Gena recognized the coat from the night of the party.

"I held on to this so I could return it to you." He smiled.

"Thank you." She retrieved the coat and stepped down the first riser.

Turning to him one last time she said, "Good night."

With a sweeping glance up and down the quiet street, she descended the steps to the sidewalk. As her toe touched the concrete, she let herself dissipate into a cloud of black mist. Thoughts of home pulled her particles in that direction and moments later she hovered in the ceiling shadows of the hallway outside her door. It was empty, and she resumed her human form, drew her key from her pocket, and entered her home.

B ayn drew a deep breath as he watched her shift and disappear.

The absence of her presence pulled at him.

After the brightness of her company, his world seemed a shade darker with her departure.

Turning to go back inside, he considered his decision to ease the mounting tension between then.

The second her magic had reacted to his own, he knew.

He knew she was the one.

Mate. His inner dragon piped up.

It *was* magic between them. And it was the right kind.

But he wanted to take it slow.

Do it right.

His body wasn't thanking him for it. He needed a cold shower after the way she'd been looking at him—mirroring his desire.

His memory replayed every nuance of her expressions, her posture, and every unconscious movement, then let his imagination take over to where he would have liked the rest of the evening to go.

In the shower, he imagined the feel of her lips on his. His tongue sweeping the satin of her skin; the taste of her magic and her essence. He grew harder in his lathered hand, caressing himself as he imagined caressing the full curves of her lush body. He spilled himself, releasing some of the tension in his body, but it wasn't enough.

He wanted Gena. He needed her.

Despite knowing now she was his mate, he wanted her to truly know it too.

Early the following morning, he instructed his assistant Kaylie to reach out to Gena with the contract proposition details he'd had in mind.

There was a substantial estate going to auction and he was handling the appraisal. It wasn't a typical estate auction, though. The property and its contents had belonged to a very good, long-time friend who'd recently passed. She'd been a business partner for decades and had very specific instructions on how she wanted her estate handled. In the business for decades, collecting had been her passion; she'd kept everything strictly itemized and had vertical files of cataloging and digitizing.

"Make sure the proposal includes the attachment with the list of special items, along with known property details that require the most dedicated research for the project." Bayn instructed his assistant. "The history will be published with the proceeds going to the local historical society."

"Yes, sir," she answered, and rose to get the files needed from the cabinet on what to include. "What is the estimated time line?"

"I'll give her a week to decide, but I expect the project to be lengthy. Six to twelve months at least."

The assistant nodded and settled back in front of her screen.

Leaving her to it, he went into his office and settled in to work on open accounts, but his mind kept drifting back to Gena—hoping she'd confirm soon.

Hoping she wouldn't decline.

Hoping he'd see her soon.

His imagination brought him a vision of her wandering through his office, working right there with him.

That would be perfect!

He wondered if he could convince her to join him in person, rather than continue remotely.

He got up and poked his head out of the door, "And tell her we can offer her work space."

The assistant's brows shot up as she looked around. It wasn't like they had spare rooms that sat empty—except for his public meeting space. "If she accepts, we'll set up the board room for her use."

The assistant shrugged and got back to work.

Was that giddiness that rippled through his chest?

He was too old for giddy.

He smiled, returning to his desk.

Yes, this was going to work out perfectly.

Conrad tuned out the auctioneer's calls to focus on the next item in the catalog. It was an exquisite piece, a sixteenth century Ming vase that he knew his adversary was there to bid on. Still deliberating on whether he wanted to outbid him just for the sake of it, he glanced across the room to where he was seated.

He'd been outbidding the old fucker at these auctions for decades now. That will teach him for screwing with something that was his. And he didn't even have to waste magic to do it.

What else was he going to do with all the time on his hands?

He turned to look at the couple whispering behind him, giving them an arch look. The woman ignored his glare, pulling her partner's attention to an antiques magazine in her hands.

She murmured a familiar name and he turned his eyes back to the items on the front pedestal while he eavesdropped on their continued conversation.

"Bai Yun Long is preparing a show up in Toronto for the estate of Elyssia Wright. I've heard rumors that the pieces in the collection are breath taking."

Conrad missed her companion's response, but she continued. "Yes, some of the funds will be funneled back into Elyssia's foundation. Apparently this has turned into a large project. He's hired a researcher to develop companion books detailing the history of the estate. And he's so invested in the project, I heard he might add some of his own pieces to the auction catalog to boost the charitable funds."

His own collection.

Finally. Words he'd been traveling to these events for years to hear. Following Long's career in the antiquities field for decades, he'd never once heard of him selling his own collection. Always acquisitions. A frisson rippled through him.

He turned back to the couple. "Excuse me, where did you acquire that magazine? The one with the article on the Elyssia Wright estate?"

She told him the title and issue number.

He rose and left the auction mid-bidding war, the Ming forgotten.

Chapter Six

Gena stared at the email. Again.

She had until the end of today to send a response.

The first time she had opened it, her excitement had soared while reading it. Until she reached the final lines offering her own work space at his office.

Terror ripped through her.

Working with him in close quarters for six to twelve months.

She stared at that line again, now on the final day. He'd given her a week to accept the offer.

She wanted to do the project. She wanted to work with him.

But Gena usually worked alone, from the comfort of her home.

She swallowed. She wanted to spend the time with him, but what if suddenly spending that much time so close together went terribly wrong? She wasn't a 'people' person.

She didn't know if she could do this. No matter how much she had changed in the last centuries, she hadn't changed *that* much.

She just didn't do 'people'.

People were exhausting.

But Bayn wasn't 'people'. He was Bayn. Super hot and intense Bayn.

Bayn, who'd held onto her coat for months in order to return it to her one day.

She sighed and dropped her head into her hands, fingers clutching at the thick dark strands of her hair.

Her phone buzzed.

Her eyes slid to the illuminated screen. It was Olivia.

Eyes popping wide, she snatched it up.

"Hello?"

"I just got your message. You're accepting the job, *right?*"

Gena knew it wasn't really a question. Before she could answer, Olivia dove in again.

"Of course you are, when do you start?"

"He wants me to work on site."

"And?"

"On. Site."

"And? What's the problem?"

"Liv, I'm a work from home kind of girl. You know this."

"You can change."

"I don't want to. I like working from home."

"So you don't want the job and you don't like Bayn?"

"You know I do on both counts."

"Clearly not enough to step out of your comfort zone."

"Ouch."

"Truth."

Gena sighed, "Okay."

"There's nothing to be afraid of; only good can come of this new adventure in your life."

"You sound so sure."

"Trust me?"

"Always."

"Good. Send your acceptance."

"Yes ma'am."

"Love you."

"Love you too, talk soon." She hung up her phone and stared at her computer screen.

Drawing a deep breath, she said to the empty room, as she often did, "I'm going to do this and

I'm going to make it work. No, I won't think too far ahead about what could happen between Bayn and me at any point in the future. We're beginning a business relationship. I'll keep it that way. I swear."

She bit her lip, fingers hovering over the keyboard.

Yes, business relationship. Platonic. Professional. Distanced.

It didn't matter how hot her dreams had become in the six nights since their coffee date.

Memories of her past life floated up from their sunken place at the bottom of her consciousness.

Having existed in that lamp for as long as she did, she'd grown so used to being alone. Observing from her limited capacity. As the memories of her time in Bayn's hoard sped to the surface, a bubble of pressure made her heart ache.

She'd been infatuated with him for...she had no idea how long.

Nor had she any idea why she'd been so infatuated. That hadn't happened with any of the other owners of her lamp.

Her face stung with embarrassment. She wasn't that person anymore. Not for a long,

long time. So why did these old feelings and habits keep coming back?

She had to examine those past emotions and put them back in the past, where they belonged.

Focus on now. Focus on the work she now did and loved. And she did love the work she chose to do. It occupied her mind and fed her thrill of the hunt. Ask questions, solve the puzzles, put them in place, and make the story whole again.

Olivia had once suggested she document the history of her own lamp—and her own long existence. That doing so might help bring perspective and closure in some way.

Gena didn't like the idea of inspecting her own past so closely. She'd never outright refused though. Just said, 'maybe' and left it at that.

Besides, the life of a djinn was incredibly boring. Long, long periods of solitary nothingness in the confines of the lamp, with short bouts of hyper-activity as she was roused and summoned to work her magic.

But *those* times...she supposed there were stories in *those* times. Of *those* people.

Some of them didn't deserve the digital characters required to type the words to say they existed. But others, some were sweet and kind. Like Olivia.

Her Olivia. Her heart swelled. Olivia, her savior. Gena's freedom was granted at her hands. She was special. Now that woman deserved a tome for all that she'd accomplished in her long lifetime.

Perhaps it was time Gena started trying to live up to the life that had been given back to her. Make it worthwhile. Do something with it—like actually live it.

Maybe even give back to the world?

She wasn't so sure about that.

She'd given plenty.

Having lived the life of a djinn, shackled to a lamp, where anyone could make demands of her, she'd given plenty.

Most plentiful had been her magic and her life itself. Being forced to use it to do things that she abhorred, but had no way not to do. Whatever the wish, she'd had to fulfill it.

Olivia had used her wish—her one wish—to give Gena her freedom.

The only thing she'd ever asked in return was that one gift; to grant one wish to Quinn O'Clery.

That one request, to give a gift to Quinn, had led her straight to Bayn again.

The dragon whom Olivia had taken her lamp from in the first place.

How ironic. She couldn't understand it.

Shaking her head to clear it of the cyclical thoughts, she stared at the email once more.

She typed her acceptance and hit send.

Done.

Then she got up to find her favorite bottle of Monarch white wine and have a glass or three.

Conrad curled his lip as he passed through Pearson airport, cutting through meandering throngs of travelers to his ride, waiting outside the main doors. The slam of the car door blocked out the deafening hum of the place. After a deep breath, he barked the name of the hotel and settled back on the leather.

He smiled, scrolling through his emails.

He almost had the bastard in his cross-hairs. After confirmation of his location, the real work would begin.

Knowing where his lair was would make it easier for him to develop his plan to take back his lamp.

He'd been searching for it for so very long and now, after centuries, it was almost his. Just a little longer. She would be his again.

He imagined she'd be unchanged. Had Bayn ever used her magic for himself?

What would a beast such as he even desire, that he could not attain himself?

Wasted. She was wasted in his possession.

It was good that he was close to finding her. She belonged with him.

Alluring eyes and lush lips, how eager she'd been to please him. To serve him. How lonely she must have been without him. He sighed, recalling their long nights and how she'd pleased him.

Poor darling must be mad from centuries without him.

He would ease her suffering.

Bayn stood in the door to his office, behind his assistant's desk. A slow smile lifted his face as Gena closed the door and turned, her glance sweeping the space.

Kaylie greeted Gena with a friendly welcome, not having seen him standing behind her.

He moved forward, drawing her attention, "Thanks Kaylie, I'll take it from here."

Startled, Kaylie moved aside.

Remembering his manners, he introduced his assistant to Gena, recalling they'd all be working very closely together.

Kaylie's eyebrows remained close to her hairline as she regarded him, then finally smiled at Gena. "Well, since Mr. Long is determined to welcome you himself, I'll just get out of the way. I'll be in my little domain if you need anything."

"Thank you." Gena answered, her voice warm and smile genuine.

That unfamiliar giddiness rolled through his chest again and he cleared his throat to stomp it back into place before proffering a hand to indicate Gena should precede him into the office he'd had converted for her.

The meeting room was larger than his own office, as it had to contain the boardroom table for larger meetings. Kaylie had helped him move the filing cabinets containing Elyssia Wright's collection, which was substantial. A desk, computer and whatever else she needed were all in place.

Looking about the room, she nodded and smiled, "this is very nice, thank you, Mr. Long."

"Call me Bayn. We look forward to the next weeks and months working with you; we want you to be comfortable." He smiled at her, eyes twinkling.

They stood, side by side, looking out over the Toronto skyline toward the setting sun, glinting off rooftops and high rises, casting its rosy glow over the lake.

Her eyes swept the room, "This is much more than I'm used to. I hope I don't get so distracted staring out the window all day that I don't get the work completed." She laughed.

"I'm sure the novelty will wear off in a day or two."

"I don't know about that," she said, her voice soft as she watched the people and traffic far below them.

"Shall we get started?"

Turning with a nod, she seemed relieved to turn her focus to the work at hand.

He began by going into more detail on the project, allowing her to ask questions on vision and development.

Falling into the familiar, they both relaxed.

The opening hour went smoothly and easily.

Every day was much the same, comfortable and filled with the day's work. Gena would arrive and Bayn would greet her like he did his assistant each day. Most often they worked in their separate spaces, had meetings, and diverged again.

Gena was incredibly professional in her dealings with him. Over the weeks, he'd watched her change a little each day. Ultra-professional and reserved throughout the first week, it wasn't until mid-way through the second week that she began to relax. There'd been a distance between them, almost as though she was determined to keep them from touching each other—especially in Kaylie's presence. Some days Gena went to lunch with Kaylie, but mostly she kept to herself.

Bayn had tried to lure her to dinner, or an after work walk, but she'd declined and made her way home again.

One morning, late in the third week, she appeared with a deep frown, which immediately set him on edge. The drive to find out what was bothering her overwhelmed him, after so long trying to keep his distance and give her the space she seemed to need.

It hadn't been easy, and his inner dragon hadn't liked being set aside for workplace correct behavior.

"Gena?"

Distracted, she didn't appear to hear him right away. He stood in the doorway of her office and called her name again.

Blinking, she looked up and focused on his face.

"Are you alright?" he asked, stepping in and closing the door behind him.

Kaylie hadn't yet arrived, but with the glass walls dividing the offices from the reception area, she'd see they were both in.

"Yes. I-uhm. I'm not sure." She looked up at him, her eyes large and glossy.

He was instantly beside her, and concern had set his heart thumping.

"Has someone done something?"

"Uhm, no. No, I don't think so." She answered with vague uncertainty. "I think I'm ill."

"Oh," he said, not sure how to process this. "Have you been ill before?" Bayn had never been ill in his life; he had no concept of what it meant or felt like.

She shook her head.

Should he call a doctor? Could a doctor help a djinn? No, of course not—could they? She did have human part of her, after all.

He offered to make the call, but she emphatically declined.

"I won't be inspected by anyone. I can't risk someone finding out what I am. Not ever again."

He sucked in a breath.

He too, kept his true nature hidden from the world, but he didn't live under any kind of threat like she did. It hadn't occurred to him before.

"Is this why you stay alone so much? To hide?"

She turned pleading eyes to him. His heart ached.

"I don't want to return to the life of a lamp djinn."

"But I thought Olivia freed you?"

"She did. But I can't risk someone figuring out how to put me back."

He stared at her in shock. "I thought once you were free, it was permanent."

"I— I don't know. Not for sure."

"Well, how do we find out for sure?" His pulse pounded in his ears and his dragon snarled as the wedge of fear for her safety leveraged itself in his chest. "Isn't your lamp destroyed?"

She shook her head again.

He stared at her, at a loss for words.

"I'd have thought you'd have destroyed it as soon as you were free."

She looked away, her head dipping. "It's complicated."

"Complicated? How can it be complicated?" he said, voice rising. He drew a breath to calm himself.

But when she turned her face back to him, her lips were set. "It's complicated." She repeated.

Clearly.

"Alright then, why don't we call Olivia? She freed you, maybe she can help us figure out what's wrong with you?" He hesitated. "What *is* wrong with you, by the way? What do you mean by *ill*?"

"My magic is fading. The last couple of days, when I teleport, I reassemble my body feeling nauseous and dizzy."

"That can't be good. What do you think is causing it?"

"I've never teleported so much as I have since I started working here. All the commuting—I think it may be getting to me."

"I had no idea your magic would, or could, deplete."

"I wasn't sure, but it seems maybe it can," she said with a dejected shrug. "I'm not sure what to do. I don't know if my magic is connected to the lamp entirely. I don't even know if I can replenish it. Or if, now that I'm no longer enslaved to it, it will just one day run out and I'll be completely human."

He considered this.

He knew little about djinns. Obviously. When he'd had one, he hadn't even known she was in his treasure trove. How did one become a djinn?

"Were you always a djinn? How does it work?"

Her expression turned pained. His gut twisted at asking her questions she clearly didn't want to answer.

Was there a society of djinns? How many were there in the world? Did they only exist in lamps? How many were ever freed? Question upon question steam-rolled him as he stared at her.

"You're staring. Please stop."

He quickly slid his gaze to the windows. "There has to be someone that can help you. Someone that knows what this means."

She held up her open hands, "I have no idea. I mean, I've been living among the humans for a number of centuries now, mostly keeping to myself and using very little magic. Between those two things it's not like I meet many people, let alone other djinn. Or other paranormals, for that matter."

A twang of sadness poked at him.

Loneliness.

He understood that. And he didn't keep himself nearly as isolated as she seemed to.

"It's time you did."

"What?"

"Meet others. Other paranormals, especially."

"No— I can't." Her beautiful large dark eyes widened in panic.

"You will, but first I have a solution to the commuting problem. You'll just stay with me."

"What?" she said, jumping to her feet. "N-no."

"Yes. I have a spare room. You called me a gentleman yourself. And I don't ravish princesses as sacrifice."

Her eyes narrowed on him. "Was that a joke?"

"May have been a poor one, but yes."

Her shoulders eased and she smiled.

"Okay, maybe for tonight. If I'm well again in the morning, I'll go back home, or find a new temporary place here."

His dragon hummed. She was going to be living closer. He'd have more time to work on her. Make her comfortable to hang out, and not run off home every night.

He'd missed her easy company since their coffee date. Not that work had been strained, particularly. Just...work.

He rubbed his hands together, which caused her to raise a brow.

She eyed him with suspicion, "What nefarious thing are you plotting?"

"Nefarious?" He flashed her a grin. "Dinner."

"Dinner?" she said.

"Yes, I'm going to cook you dinner tonight."

Her other brow rose to meet the first. "You cook?"

"Of course I do. I don't just go out stealing and eating livestock every night. That gets boring. Harder to spice when they're running and wriggling." He winked, drawing a laugh from her.

"Alright then. I'd better pajama shop during my lunch hour."

"If you insist," he teased.

They both turned as they heard Kaylie make her entrance.

"Sorry I'm late," she called, hanging up her jacket, flustered. "The commute was crazy to-day—and parking was even worse!"

Bayn frowned. "Didn't you park in our lot?"

"It's closed off. I had to park on a side street several blocks away."

He frowned. He'd received no notice that the building lot would be closed for any reasons. And of course, not driving here himself, he hadn't seen it. "Make sure you submit your parking stubs to me for reimbursement."

"Okay, thanks," Kaylie said, her shoulders dropping with her relief, "That's good of you." She smiled, "I'll have to run off at lunch to plug the meter; I got stuck at a limited time one."

"I'll go with you," Gena said. I have a bit of shopping to do."

"Ooo, shopping! I like shopping, can I join?" Kaylie's face lit up.

Gena smiled, delighted, "Of course."

"Great, it's a date."

Bayn's dragon grumbled at how easily Gena gave Kaylie a date while Bayn had to work at wriggling his way into her time slots.

But he couldn't be too sulky about it. He was glad to see her being friendly and socializing, especially after how she'd mentioned her isolation not long ago.

"Take an extended lunch, I'll hold down the reception fort."

Kaylie beamed, "Thanks boss."

"Anything for my employees of the month."

With a roll of her eyes, she said, "We're your *only* employees."

He grinned back with a mischievous wink and wandered into his office to start the morning's work.

Chapter Seven

After weeks of watching and planning, Conrad was now dressed as a workman by one of the barriers blocking the entrance to the underground garage.

Careful planning had got him this far. Not using his magic had been tedious, but necessary, so that Long wouldn't detect his presence and investigate.

Today, Conrad gaped as Long's assistant left the building with a shapely brunette he could have sworn was his djinn, from his obscured angle.

She turned, and his eyes caressed her delicate profile.

But it couldn't be her. He blinked. Too long at work, too many hours with nothing but her on his mind, and he was beginning to see her everywhere.

Suppressing the urge to reach out with his magic, he ripped the work overalls and construction vest off and tossed them aside, "Going to lunch," he barked at his coworker and left without acknowledgment, following the women.

In and out of shops they went, and he followed. No matter how much he told himself that she should still be locked away in her lamp, he could not shake the whisper that this was indeed his djinn, free and walking the streets of downtown Toronto, lingerie shopping with a colleague.

The longer he followed them down the shopping district and into the large mall, the more his disbelief deepened into a feeling of betrayal. Who the fuck had let her out? How dare she walk free without his say so? And she'd never sought him out?

She had no right. She was his djinn slave, his property. She belonged in that fucking lamp between his palms. She was his to control.

Fists curled as he stalked after them, a mall security guard stepped into his path. The guard was a very large human, much larger than his slight self. He glanced after the woman, oblivious to his presence.

"Sir, I suggest you find somewhere else to be." The guard moved so that his wide shoulders blocked Conrad's view of his djinn.

Power flared on the edge of his fingertip to send the behemoth sailing out of his way, but he caught himself.

Not the time and place. He'd learned that over the centuries. A little bit of self-control went a long way. Especially dressed as he was.

The guard waved a hand toward the mall exit with a meaningful stare.

Conrad said nothing.

That was alright. She was with Long's assistant. They'd have to go back to the office building sooner or later. It would give him time to think this through.

Now he knew she was around. This would be so much easier than breaking into Long's lair to retrieve his lamp.

He could focus on his djinn instead.

Gena's hands were clammy as she followed Bayn back to his place again.

She was a ball of nerves and excitement rolled into a coiled mess.

But she felt safe with him. She wasn't sure there was anywhere other than Olivia's place she could go where she felt easy enough to leave her apartment for a night.

She'd have to make it clear, that it was only for one night.

She watched him strut into his house, waving a hand grandly for her to enter as he held the door open for her. Then he plucked her shopping and laptop bags from her hands. "Don't take your coat off just yet, we're going out again."

"I thought we were cooking tonight?"

"We are. But we have to go pick the ingredients up first. It won't take long."

She smiled.

He seemed quite enthusiastic about the prospect.

Gena usually ordered her groceries on-line and had them delivered, or she ventured into the grocery stores at their quietest hours.

Leaving Bayn's brick townhouse, they wandered the narrow street toward the busy main road, lined with shops and restaurants. So many people were out in the few hours after the end of the work day, rushing here and there, fetching the evening dinner, as they were, and running other errands.

Each time they passed a crowd of people, she found herself walking closer and closer to Bayn, so that she ended up pressed to his arm.

He glanced down at her with a warm smile, slipping an arm around her shoulders to create a buffer until they crossed the street to the small market he guided them to.

She wandered the narrow aisles behind him as he selected various items and dropped them into his basket.

"Is there anything you'd like?"

She smiled and shook her head, content to look at everything. She was impressed with the aisle completely dedicated to sauces and flavorings of all kinds, for a wide range of palates. Her mouth watered when they passed the glassed-in hot display of roasted duck and pork. At the back of the shop, she helped him select some sweet buns before they went to look at the fresh fish.

Returning to his home, he insisted she settle on the sofa and relax while he brought her a glass of wine and began the preparations.

Gena would never have imagined Bayn, of all beings, cooking dinner for her.

Simply, no one ever had, really.

She'd had dinner with Olivia's family, but that was usually a group event.

After a time, feeling awkward sitting alone in the living room with just his paintings and art to keep her company, she picked up her wine glass and wandered into the back of the house, seeking out the kitchen.

Everything was crisp and sleek, with highly polished lines of counter and cabinetry in this century old townhouse.

"So, tell me," she began, drawing his attention as he prepped a pan for the filleted and seasoned fish. "What did you do with it all? Basement vault with high security?"

He grinned at her from the island where he worked. "Something like that." He moved to check the pot of rice and steaming vegetables before placing the fillets in the pan.

They stopped speaking as the fish crackled loudly in the oil, steam billowing up into the overhead fan. She watched him work, the aroma of the food filling the space and making her stomach growl.

She took advantage of the break in talking to just watch him.

He'd exchanged his work clothes for jeans and a long sleeved shirt, pushed up his forearms. A black cooks' apron protected him from the splatter of the searing oil.

She sipped her wine as her eyes drank him in. The pan looked incredibly heavy, but he moved it like it was plastic, lifting and shuffling the fish along its surface. His movements smooth, her presence seemed forgotten, lost in the activity of cooking.

He'd clearly been doing this for a long time. Lifetimes?

She wondered what he'd done with himself after Olivia's crash interception of his lofty golden treasure-hoarding life.

Probably a hell of a lot more than she had been doing. She sighed and put her wine down on the counter, losing herself in his movements. Was this domestic contentment?

Or was it just a novelty for her? As new as this moment was for her, it clearly was routine for him. He was part of this world now, whereas she still struggled on its fringes.

Could she become part of it too? Be as easy in the world among humans as he was?

Did she want to be?

He glanced up at her and grinned.

She swallowed, absorbing the shiver his grin caused to ripple through her.

She wanted to be in his world.

Part of it, this time. Not just a distant voyeur.

For him to know she was in it.

He slid the aromatic fish onto two plates with steaming dark green vegetables and fluffy white rice and carried them to the small dining table. Picking up the wine and glasses, she wandered over, seeing he'd already set it before she'd joined him in the kitchen.

"Smells fabulous." She inhaled with a smile.

"Wait till you taste it."

She settled in beside him so they shared a corner of the table, instead of directly across from him. This was much more intimate.

He poured more wine into her glass and waited for her to take the first bites, watching her face intently.

Placing a slice of the fish on her tongue, her mouth exploded with flavor and she closed her eyes with a moan. "I've never tasted anything so good."

"I've had a lot of time to perfect my recipe." He smiled, tucking into his own plate.

"This is so good. I'm used to just making quick meals or having delivery." She glanced up to see the horror on his face. "What? What's wrong?"

"You're joking."

"No, why?"

"You can't live an eternity like that."

She shrugged and bit into the garlic infused vegetables with another groan. "I may just hire you to be my cook." She licked the juices from her lips and dabbed the napkin to her mouth.

"Nonsense, you can just move in with me and I'll cook for you all the time."

She laughed, "That could get old pretty fast; you'd be tired of me in three days."

"Is that a challenge?" The look he gave her held a serious glint in his eye.

She swallowed, her pulse steadily increasing the longer he stared at her. Images of living here with him rolled through her mind.

She blinked and sipped her wine.

"We have dessert?"

"We sure do," he said softly, as his expression relaxed into a secretive grin. He rose from his place and was back seconds later with one of the sweet buns cut into pieces. He placed the plate between them and set another smaller dipping bowl to the side.

Leaning over to see better, the smaller bowl held a smooth black paste. "What is it?"

"Black sesame." He picked up a small piece of the flaky white bun, dipped a small edge of it into the paste, and held it up to her lips.

The sweet smell of the dessert tickled her nose as she looked at his expectant expression.

She dropped her eyes to his fingers as they moved closer to her mouth. She could pluck it from him, but she opened her lips and let him deposit it on her tongue. As her mouth closed, she suckled his fingertips with a light tongue swipe.

She grinned when he sucked in a breath.

The dessert melted over her tongue.

"Oh my, that is good."

She mimicked his movements, picking up a piece and dipping it in the sweet black paste, then held it for him. He took it with his lips, as she had done, but caught her hand as he chewed and swallowed. He licked and nibbled the errant crumbs from her fingers, letting his nose glide along the inside of her wrist.

A shiver rippled the rest of the way up her arm. Her nipples hardened with the first curls of desire. When he returned his gaze to her, she sucked in her breath at the intensity of his expression.

He looked as though he wanted to devour her, too.

He leaned across the corner of the table that separated them.

She licked her lips and met him.

His lips were warm. Salty sweet from their dinner. Bayn's tongue flicked against the corner of her mouth. Granting him entrance, she gasped as the probe of his tongue sent a shock of desire straight down to her core.

She pulled away to catch her breath. Her eyes swept the strong lines of his tanned face, down the column of his throat to his wide shoulders. She wanted to put her hands on those shoulders. To palm his biceps and smooth pecs, and abs... those too. Her gaze dropped to his hips, really wanting his shirt off. She imagined every line of his body in the perfect symmetry of his wiry physique.

Power.

Not the muscle-bound kind. Inner power. Total physical control, every muscle honed with purpose.

He was intense, and she suspected he attacked every aspect of his life with that same intensity.

Work. Cooking. Exercise. Loving.

Her breath hitched.

He still watched her face. Patience. His eyes glimmered with his inner intensity, but he was patient as she made up her mind.

The last couple of weeks she'd kept a professional distance between them.

What the hell for?

She couldn't remember why.

He'd respected that space and matched her professionalism, but she had seen how he'd looked at her. The heated, unguarded looks when Kaylie wasn't in the room. Every moment together layered inside of her. A light dusting of her desire for him building and building.

Drawing a shaky breath, she glanced down and dipped her fingertip into the black sesame sauce, then lightly drew it across the inside of his lower lip, following it with her tongue.

He growled, tongue sweeping hers, claiming her. Her hands sought his face, frustrated with the table corner separating them.

She wanted to be in his lap where she could taste him properly.

As though sensing what she wanted, she somehow found herself swept up onto his lap. Thighs straddling his, she looked down into his dark eyes. Heat radiated from his taut body, but she was even hotter for him. Glancing up at her, his left hand kneaded her hip while his right slid up her waist and gently massaged her breast before pinching the buttons of her blouse to release her from the confines of her clothes.

Loving the way he looked at her, she surprised herself in wanting to reveal more to him. Blouse open, he placed gentle kisses on her exposed flesh along the edge of her lacy bra. His lips nibbled and tongue swirled, finding her nipple through the fabric. Her head fell back as he explored her breasts.

Pushing her shirt down, she released her bra. He sighed, "Beautiful."

The tip of his nose slid over the peak of a nipple. Turning his head, he found the small sauce bowl and dipped his finger into it, then drew little circles over each of her nipples. Her breath shuddered as he licked the sweet stuff away.

The absence of his mouth on her skin drew her attention back to his face as he stared at her, eyes sweeping her face. He waited until she was looking at him before letting his fingers drift up her spread thighs to the hem of her skirt.

Holding her gaze, they slipped under the edge, very slowly gliding along her flesh to the edge of her undergarment, then stopped again.

Gena stared at him as she struggled to control her breathing.

He waited.

She realized he was waiting for her to decide.

Decide to stop there or continue on.

Reaching for his face, she kissed him with all the pent up passion she'd been suppressing for weeks.

With a growl, he was on his feet, taking her with him as his arm swept their dishes to the far end of the table, clearing the space for his real dessert.

Her bottom hit the surface as he gently laid her back across it. Bending over her, he reveled in her body a moment longer before returning to her face.

Staring up into his intense eyes, his hair falling loose about his forehead, she ran her fingers through the silky strands, pulling his mouth to hers again as her ankles pulled him closer against her hot core.

He was hard. So hard.

And she throbbed, wanting—needing—him to fill her.

He eased back, hands sliding down her torso. Settling back onto his chair, he pushed her skirt up to her hips, then hooked his fingers into her panties and slid them down so that she hid nothing from him.

Raised on her elbows, she looked down into his face as his eyes devoured her.

He licked his lips.

She held her breath.

As he'd done with her breasts, he kissed first one inner thigh, then the other.

When his gaze returned to her heated face he grinned again, the mischief returning. The chill of something wet touched her hot core and she realized he'd painted her intimate parts with the black sesame paste.

Her pent breath blew out and was sucked back in with a gasp as his head lowered again. The first tentative swirls of his tongue on her nub made her drop her head back in a haze.

She couldn't believe this was happening.

Was it another dream?

Glancing down at his head, it certainly didn't feel like a dream. It was so much better.

His fingers slid in and out as his mouth worked her over.

Eyes closed, the haze turned white and she soared as her body shuddered.

With a final sweep of his tongue, the tip of his nose slid along the sensitive flesh of her inner thigh before he planted a gentle kiss on it.

She had no words as she stared down the length of her body.

He looked as sated as she felt.

His lips quirked as he stood and held out a hand to help her to her feet. Chest still heaving, her legs wobbled as he pulled her against his chest for support. His length was a solid bar against her hip.

Reaching down, she caressed him, but he caught her hand, kissing her palm.

"What about you?"

"Not tonight." He planted a light kiss on her mouth.

Once she caught her balance, he pressed her wine glass to her hand to occupy her hands while he fixed her clothing for her.

She stared, dumbfounded.

"I'll show you to your room, so you can relax the rest of the evening. Do you want a bath?"

She'd died and gone to the heavens.

Surely she must have been hit by a bus while they were out shopping, and this was her afterlife.

Bayn showered. Again.

Gena's scent lingered, imprinted. Her soft moans and sighs burned into his memory.

He smiled, recalling how unsteady she'd been on her feet after his dessert feast. Her cheeks flushed, with swollen lips and heaving chest as she stared at him. Her confusion, as she tried to return his caresses and was refused.

There would be time for that later.

For now, he was content having finally tasted her.

Beyond the office environment, he'd finally been able to tease the passion out of her. Made her moan with wanton abandon on his table.

Best dessert ever.

So good.

She had him so hard.

His hand squeezed around his cock as he came again.

He smiled, knowing he'd been the one to drive her to it. And he looked forward to burying himself deep inside of her hot little core.

However, he was going to make damned sure she was ready for him.

When he claimed her, she was going to know it.

And she was going to claim him in return.

Bayn flipped the last of the pancakes and switched off the burner. Gena approached, bare feet quiet on the hardwood floor of the hall. He grinned at the muscle-bound blue genie covering the front of her night shirt. "Hungry?"

"Famished." Her eyes swept the dishes laid out on the table where he'd... Her eyes slipped back to his face as heat infused her cheeks and chest.

He chuckled, helping her with her chair.

He piled her plate with pancakes, bacon and fresh fruit, then handed her the syrup. "Go nuts."

Eyes wide, she giggled like a child as she tipped the bottle end over nib with two hands and watched the golden ooze layer the pancakes. "I'm drooling." She licked her lips.

Me too.

He watched her dig into the food. She moaned as her lips closed over her fork.

"I think we should take the day off."

Her eyes popped open. "Why?"

"Clearly, something's going on with your magic, as you said yesterday. We should figure out what's happening."

"I was thinking about that." She waved her fork in front of her, "It's probably just the long distances and time away from the lamp. I've never been away from it longer than a few hours."

"But aren't you free?"

She shrugged. "Yeah. Mostly."

"I don't follow." He leaned forward as she looked up at the ceiling, thinking.

"Uhm, how to explain it." She chewed on a bacon slice and licked her fingers.

Feeding her was either going to drive him crazy or create a situation where they were shagging all the damned time. Every little moan and lick of her lips and tongue stirred body parts he'd nearly forgotten about. In her presence he was becoming as randy as an instinct-driven dragonling.

"Liv used her wish to free me from the lamp."

He nodded. "I remember." Not one of his better moments.

Her eyes darted to his face for a long moment. Her pensive expression eased into a gentle smile. She reached out a hand to stroke the back of his. "You didn't know."

No, he hadn't, but that didn't negate the sense of responsibility that had crashed down on him after that event.

Liv.

"There's always been part of me that hasn't been able to let it go. The lamp was part of me for so long, I don't know how to live without it." She laughed, but it was short, "Believe me, not for lack of Olivia's efforts to get me to let it go." She shrugged. "I just can't. I don't know how."

His fingers laced through hers, "I understand that."

Her eyes searched his. She nodded, seeing that he truly did.

"It takes time," he said.

Her eyes glistened as she nodded, "It's been centuries. And I still haven't been able to let it go." She drew a deep shuddering breath. "I'm afraid if I let it go I'll lose something. Lose part of myself. Or worse; someone else could claim it and use it against me. It's the vessel for my magic, but it's also all I have left of my father. He made it for me."

"Hey," he said, his voice soft as he tugged her fingers so that she moved to his lap. "I won't let anyone use it against you ever again."

"You know how to prevent it?"

"We'll figure it out together. Besides, I'll bet Olivia knows someone that can help."

"I haven't wanted to bother her with it. She's been trying for decades. She has her own life to worry about."

"Has your magic returned since yesterday?"

Still perched on his lap, she closed her eyes and held up her fingers. A sad little flame appeared and sputtered like a guttering tea light. Opening them again she shook her head, her lips tight. "I don't think I have enough left to go home." Her voice shook. "Even if I take the train back, what am I going to do? There's still so much work to do on the project. We're on track to meet the deadline comfortably."

"You can stay here."

"But the lamp is alone in my apartment."

"Does anyone know it exists?"

She shook her head. "I don't think so. My apartment is warded, but I can't guarantee the wards will hold if I lose my magic completely.

"That settles it then. Despite there being plenty of open farmland and forest between Toronto and Ottawa, I can't risk shifting into my dragon form to fly you there. So, road trip it is."

She giggled. "That would be quite the sight."

"And a hell of a ride." He winked.

Chapter Eight

"Are you sure about this?" Gena asked as they sped along the highway, headed east out of Toronto in Bayn's car.

"Absolutely. Kaylie said she'd 'hold down the fort'."

"I mean about me staying in your place."

"Again, absolutely. Are you?"

She drew in a deep breath. "No."

He shot her a glance as he navigated around a transport truck. Once settled back in the center lane, he reached out and grasped her fingers. "It'll be okay."

Studying his profile, again, it was like her eyes couldn't get enough of him. And after last night, the yearning for him was settling into her. Dropping her eyes to their entwined hands, her heart jumped. She couldn't believe this was happening, no matter that she'd wanted to avoid it.

She was terrified of wanting this. To entertain the thought of allowing herself to feel something for someone—for real—again.

Her chest shuddered as she drew another deep breath to control the flip of her thoughts. Turning her face toward her window, the blue-gray haze of Lake Ontario slid by.

Could she trust him?

Could she trust herself?

He wasn't Conrad.

She peeked at him again while his focus was on the road ahead. Black hair with a slight wave, deeply tanned skin, a smooth angular jaw below high cheek bones. Her gaze landed on the corner of his mouth. She licked her lips, resisting the urge to kiss him. He was a powerful magnet and she was fractured shards of iron, drawn to him.

She always had been. Time hadn't changed that.

As though feeling her gaze, he glanced in her direction again. "What is it? Is there syrup on my face?"

"No." She smiled. "Just thinking."

"Of?"

"The past."

"Oh." His voice flattened. "We've got a few hours with nothing else to do, may as well talk about it."

"What's there to say?"

"How about, I was such a greedy bastard, I didn't even know I had a living being trapped in a lamp in my hoard?"

"That's harsh."

"But true." He shrugged.

"I can see that you've changed a lot since then. It's obvious in the way you live."

"Maybe, but some habits are still hard to break."

Her heart sped up. Was this a mistake?

"I still want you in my lair." He grinned as he looked at her.

Heart pounding now, she tried to filter what he meant from what her fear whispered.

Seeing her expression, his smile faded.

There was an OnRoute service station coming up and he pulled into the lot to park the car. He turned it off and turned in his seat to face her directly.

"Gena?" he asked, his dark eyes searching her face.

"It may be best if you just leave me at my place. Go back to Toronto without me and I'll work remotely."

"Why?" His black brows lowered into a frown. "Clearly I said something that upset you."

She tried to smile and lie. "Not at all."

His frowned deepened into a scowl as he thought about what he'd just said. "I think I might understand. You're afraid I want your lamp—your magic."

I'm terrified that you do—or will.

The fear was a yawning maw in her gut, despite her statement about seeing how much he has changed.

Her instinct whispered through the fear.

Bayn isn't Conrad.

Gena shook her head.

His expression turned skeptical.

"It's a long story." She waved her hand. Looking up at the glass and brick building, she said, "Since we're here, may as well stretch our legs."

She got out of the car before he could push the subject.

Bayn watched her leap out of his car in an effort to get away from him.

It was all over her face. She didn't trust him.

Was it any wonder? She'd spent centuries trapped in servitude to the greedy and the power hungry.

Self-disgust rolled through him again. He glanced at her through the windshield. She leaned on the fender, waiting for him.

He got out and approached her. Moving in close he reached for her face. She stood motionless as she let him kiss her.

He could feel it. He knew he felt how much she wanted him. But now that he was paying more attention, he could also sense her fear.

He pulled away, hands holding her delicate face between his palms.

Lips parted, she opened her eyes.

His chest tightened at seeing how glassy her eyes were, before she quickly blinked away unshed tears.

He needed to slow down. Give her time.

They were eternal. They had all the time in the world.

Though if she lost her magic, she would become human. Mortal.

A human lifespan was a breath compared to a dragon's.

And he'd just found her. After all this time, he'd finally found his mate.

He didn't understand the connection between her and the lamp. He wouldn't care about it, except that he realized it somehow affected her well-being.

"I'm going to call Olivia."

Gena frowned. "What for?"

"To figure this out."

Bayn's nostrils twitched, his attention pulled toward another section of the parking lot. There was another paranormal here. Muted magic. Hard to pinpoint, but still powerful enough to detect.

"What is it?" Gena asked.

"Nothing," he said, turning his full attention back to her lovely face. "A short walk, then back on the road." He kissed her forehead and brushed the pads of his thumbs over her cheekbones.

So lovely.

He wanted her to claim him.

He'd have to let her see she could trust him.

Conrad stood by his car watching his djinn with the dragon.

He seethed.

She belonged to him.

Mine.

If she's been under the dragon's dominion all this time, how much of it was spent as lovers?

She looked as though she couldn't get out of that car fast enough and he pursued her, kissing her. Marking her as his territory.

It didn't matter.

Conrad would take her back.

He turned away from the couple as the dragon's head turned in his direction.

Shit.

Did he know he was there?

Conrad was powerful and old, but he wasn't so sure he was powerful enough to defeat a dragon. Not without help. Not without the help of djinn power.

First he'd have to get to her. Convince her to go with him—if she could. Where was her lamp?

He may have to retrieve the lamp. Take it from the dragon.

He waited till they went inside the service center to approach their car. He moved toward it as though he were just going to admire the sleek Tesla. With another quick glance to ensure they were out of sight, he twisted his fingers, using his magic to bypass the alarm and trigger the locks. There was nothing on the backseat or floors. The trunk was likewise bare.

Where the fuck was the lamp?

He pressed a little harder with his power, searching for it by its magical signature, but found nothing. Just traces of the dragon and his djinn, but hers was weak. He frowned, closing up the vehicle, and went back toward his own car to think.

He paced.

Surely it was hidden back at the dragon's place, if it wasn't close to her.

If that were the case, how could she be this far from it for so long, and clearly not heading back any time soon?

What was going on?

He looked to the service station. Could he intercept her?

Jogging to the glass doors, he slipped inside. With a quick twist of his fingers he threw up a shield to mute his magic from the dragon, or any other paranormals that might be close by.

He'd already been careless leaving the shield down for so long, but the absence of the lamp had thrown him.

Raising the hood of his jacket, he scanned the open food court.

Not seeing her, his fingers flicked through the various items in his coat pocket, selecting a dime. He cast another surreptitious glance, murmured several words, and pinched the tiny coin.

Now he just had to find her. He wasn't sure how the dragon would react to his presence—probably not favorably.

His breath hitched with excitement.

There she was.

He focused on her face and walked straight in her direction, letting the side of his body brush hers; the coin slid into her pocket. Keeping his face obscured, he held up a placating hand, "Sorry 'bout that." And kept going toward the coffee shop.

Chapter Nine

Olivia stepped forward to wrap her arms around Gena, squeezing the life out of her.

"Wow, Liv, I didn't expect you to be here so quickly," Gena said.

"Bayn mentioned you were feeling ill. What else could I do? You never get sick."

"Did you bring chicken soup?" Gena grinned at her.

"Of course," She held up a thermos, returning the grin before looking at Bayn. "Long time."

He nodded. "Too long."

Olivia gave Bayn a long hug. Her eyes were misty when she stepped away from him. "Come on then, let's get inside so we can catch up." She prodded Gena.

Setting the thermos on the counter, Olivia immediately rounded on Gena. "Symptoms?"

Gena recounted what had been happening.

"I've never heard of anything like this; let me make some calls."

"To?"

"I'll call Quinn first. She knows everyone. And she's discreet. I'm sure she can put us in touch with someone that will know how to help. Why don't you go and see if you feel any different with it nearby."

Gena's eyes darted to Bayn, but she nodded and disappeared down the hall toward her room.

"So? Things are going well with Gena?"

"Starting to, but she suddenly got skittish."

Olivia nodded, reaching a hand out to his arm. "Just be patient. Her first—and possibly only—love is the one that put her in that lamp."

"Holy fuck, you're kidding." Bayn gaped at Olivia.

"I'm not."

"That's fucked up."

"It is."

He ran a hand through his hair as he stared down the empty hall. "No wonder."

She stepped aside as she dialed Quinn's number.

"Olivia! How are you?" Her voice was strong and friendly.

"I'm great, Quinn, but I have a small favor to ask, if you can spare a few minutes?"

"Of course, ask away."

Olivia described what was happening with Gena. "Can you reach out to someone that can help her?"

"I'll see what I can do."

"Thank you so much, Quinn, this really means a lot."

"And their relationship?"

Olivia shot Bayn a glance, who she knew was listening to their conversation. "So far, mostly good?"

He reached a hand out and Olivia placed her phone in it.

"Hey Quinn, I wanted to thank you for making this possible."

They chatted for several more minutes before Bayn handed Olivia back her phone. She quickly said her own good-byes and dropped it back into her pocket as Gena returned with her lamp in hand. Her eyes on Bayn, she hesitated before placing it on the counter.

He stepped away from it and sat on a stool. "Why don't you tell me how this came to be? Maybe that will help us figure out how to fix the problem?"

Her hand slid over the gleaming lamp.

Olivia placed a hand over Gena's, catching her eyes. "It's okay, you can trust him. I told him Conrad put you in there in the first place."

Gena's cheeks turned a dark pink. "I don't like talking about it."

"I know, but this is important, Gena. It's been centuries since I used the power of your wish to grant your freedom. And yet you're still tied to it. We need to figure out why."

"Why don't you start with your life before the lamp?" Bayn suggested.

Olivia had never seen Gena look so vulnerable as she stared wide-eyed from one to the other.

Gena felt the comfort of Olivia's hand on hers.

She looked at Bayn, seated at the end of the counter, his eyes boring into her face, arms crossed.

She sighed, stomach knotting.

Bayn's voice was soft as he spoke to her. "Djinns are powerful beings. Among the most ancient. Older than dragons."

"I don't remember my early years much." She shrugged. "I existed, doing as I pleased, going where I fancied. Humans were an enigma. I do remember that. So different. Mortal. Yet like a lit tallow wick in the long dark nights. Some of them anyway." Her eyes turned to Olivia.

She mentioned the day Olivia had wished Gena her freedom. Gena had gifted her longevity for her incredible generosity.

"In those earliest days, I was young," she went on. "Naive, I suppose."

"She fell in love," Olivia said to Bayn.

Gena dropped her gaze to her hands. "I thought he loved me too. He was the first person I ever gave longevity to." Her gaze returned to Olivia's face, who nodded and offered a warm smile. Returning her gaze to Bayn, she straightened her shoulders and stumbled headlong into her tale. Olivia was the only person she'd ever told it to, so despite how much she'd relived the events in her mind, the words were awkward on her tongue.

"Conrad was learning to be a sorcerer. I found him alone in the woods practicing his magic. Curious, I engaged him." She smiled. "I wasn't shy in those days. Just the opposite. I demanded to know what a human was doing with such gifts. He told me he'd seen others do such things as he did; moving objects with his words and a wave of his hands. Drawing energy to replenish his own, pushing energy into something else.

We began as friends and then became lovers. Being immortal, we both thought it would be prudent for him to also be long-lived so we could be together always. And we were inseparable for decades as he learned his magic. I loved him more and more. I couldn't say why. I should like to think it wasn't just his handsome face and thick blond hair. There was a charm to him, a strong charisma. I enjoyed making him happy, and he seemed to thrive on it.

One day, after our love making, he brought up the subject of my name. My true name. If we were to be together always, there should be no secrets between us."

Gena's heart hammered in her chest as the emotions she'd felt all those centuries ago rolled back through her as though it were happening again in the recounting.

"My true name. My true identity. My essence. The core of my power." She drew a deep breath. "He used it to bind me to the lamp. My power, my identity, its essence, is meshed with mine."

Olivia moved away to get a glass of water, which she gave to Gena.

Gena nodded her thanks, glancing at Bayn. He remained still, stone-faced.

"To what purpose?" he asked, his voice so low she almost didn't hear him.

"Profit."

"How?"

"The purchase of one wish per client."

"Fuck!" Bayn was on his feet, hands on the counter. "I can't believe that bastard."

Startled, Gena stepped away from his outburst, but went on. "He grew very rich and renowned, until the wrong customer outsmarted him. My lamp, with me in it, was stolen. I bounced from one owner to the next, compelled to grant wishes along the way. Wish spent, I was tossed aside or sold to the next."

Bayn snarled.

Gena's lips snapped shut.

"Sorry. Please go on." He sat back on the stool.

"Until one day, I woke up in your lair."

It was his turn to look abashed. "There were raiders on the steppes that were particularly annoying, pushing into my territory. I took care of them and rewarded myself with their raided loot. I just scooped it up and dumped it all in my lair."

"I didn't mind those days. I just watched and waited. I'd never seen a dragon before."

"How bored you must have been."

"At times, when I didn't hibernate and you were absent for long periods." She shrugged, then looked at Olivia. "Then Liv came along."

"And changed us all," Bayn said, flashing her best friend a genuine smile.

Liv's fingers slid over Gena's while her other hand reached for Bayn's. "My two friends. We have to figure this out. I thought I freed you, but you've never truly been free. Not since you met this Conrad."

Bayn stood up, moving around the counter top, ignoring the lamp. His eyes were glued to Gena's face. Her heart pattered at the intensity of his dark gaze. His hand slid over her cheek. She closed her eyes, enjoying the feel of his palm on her skin.

"You need to take back your power. I don't know how. Maybe destroy the lamp, or cast a spell of your own. Make it yours. As it is, it's something that this Conrad chained to you." His attention turned back to Olivia, "We need to help her figure out how to take her true identity back from him. Sever the connection."

"I don't think I can destroy it," Gena said, head ringing at the thought. "No, I couldn't do that."

"Are you sure? I can use my dragon magic to transform the goddess-damned thing. I could do it tonight if you wanted."

She lay her hand on his, "No, I don't think so-I don't think that's a good idea." She stammered, her face flushing with anxiety.

"Okay Gena. Think about it, though," Olivia said, "I'm sure Quinn will help us find someone that will know how to sever the bond."

"In the meantime, come back home with me." Bayn said.

Goddess, she wanted to.

Her eyes landed on the lamp. She blinked as Olivia swiped it into one of Gena's over-sized purses. She smiled up at her friend, who shoved the handles over her arm and onto her shoulder.

"Go. Be somewhere other than this little apartment. Live for a while. As soon as Quinn contacts me, I'll be in touch and we'll sort this out."

Gena laughed, "Okay, but we just got here after driving half the day."

"Right. Take a nap, then go back. Maybe pack some extra clothes, too.

Nodding, Gena put the purse back on the counter and wandered back to her bedroom to collect more clothes.

Staring at her room, she realized she'd only been away for a day and a half. For some reason, in that time, something had changed in her. Her room no longer felt like her sanctuary. Catching her reflection in the closet door mirror, she hesitated.

Even if she wasn't sure she trusted Bayn—or herself—she did trust Olivia implicitly.

And Olivia was hot for Gena to return to Bayn's lair.

She suddenly wondered how much of that Christmas party invitation thing had been a set up.

Now that she thought about it, the look on Olivia's face when she had held both their hands wasn't just that of a friend relishing the bonds of friendship. There was something more there.

Gena poked her head out of the bedroom door and called, "Liv?"

A moment later Olivia entered the room. "Need help choosing stuff?"

Gena noted that Liv wandered straight for the underthings pile on her bed. "Hmm, serviceable."

She raised a brow at her friend. "Shouldn't it be?"

"Well, you know.... One should always be prepared."

"Prepared..."

Olivia's face took on a fully mischievous expression. "For sexy time, of course."

She narrowed her eyes and crossed her arms. "Liv, did you set me up, the night of the Christmas party?"

Rolling her eyes dramatically, Olivia said, "Of course I did, love. I can't believe you didn't realize that until just now. You really have spent way too much time shut up in this place."

"Did you want me to meet just anyone, or did you know Bayn would be there?"

Olivia shrugged, "I may have made a suggestion or two for the guest list."

"Liv!"

"Well it's working out, isn't it? Would have been nice if things hadn't gone cold for months and months in between, but better late than never."

"And the coffee date?"

"Not me. Him."

Gena's eyes slid to the wall that separated her room from the kitchen.

"Quinn didn't hocus pocus that?"

"I don't know how Quinn does things, but I doubt she'd 'hocus pocus' a coffee date." She thought a moment. "I bet it was that hot little red dress I talked you into."

Gena groaned and dropped onto her bed. "Why am I so dumb?"

"Awe honey, you're not dumb. You just spend too much time on your own, thinking of others all the time. It doesn't occur to you that others think of you, too."

Tears filled Gena's eyes. "How did I get here? I feel so wishy-washy and afraid all the time. I wasn't always like this." Her thoughts tumbled back to what she'd said about how fearless she'd been in her youth. Before the entrapment.

Olivia's arms came around Gena's shoulders. "Hey, look at me. You're a lovely woman. You're kind and generous."

"Yeah, look where that got me."

"Sure, it led you to that idiot Conrad. But it also led us to each other. And to Bayn. And I can tell you now, he doesn't want your power. He doesn't need it. He's a frikking dragon, Gena. Sure, he may have liked your shiny little lamp at one time, but that had nothing to do with who you are. He had no idea what a true treasure was within it."

Gena sniffled, staring at Olivia's wavering face through the building tears. "How can you know for sure?"

"After all these years, you've suddenly stopped trusting me." Olivia's voice was soft.

"I guess this time my heart's on the line again, and the fear is really, *really* high." Gena held up a hand and waved it as high as she could over her head.

"Do you want him?" she whispered.

Gena nodded, "Yes. I do."

"Then claim him."

"Just like that. You make it sound easy."

"It's not complicated."

"What if what I want isn't as much as what he wants?"

"Then, I think he'll say so, but I think he may surprise you."

"How can you know?"

Olivia tipped a shoulder coyly. "That's my super power. I *know* things."

"And this is one of *those* things?"

"Mmhmm."

"You're going to have to explain to me how that works, one of these days."

"Yeah sure, but not today. Today you have to pick all your best lacy pretty things to pack."

"I don't have many of those. I'm mostly a flannel and cotton kind of djinn."

"Don't worry, we'll find something."

Gena stared at Olivia's 'determined-face' and she knew there was no avoiding the power of Liv's mission once she was set on one. They wandered over and peered into the depths of Gena's closet.

"Mission impossible." Gena muttered.

"I chose to accept this mission."

Conrad lurked outside the djinn's apartment door, in the shadows of the hall. Once in the space, he'd been able to detect the wards she'd put in place. They were weak. He could break them in time, but instead he chose to listen in.

He tapped into the scrying magic he had placed on the dime, which seemed to have remained in her coat pocket since he had dropped it in there, back at the service center.

Eyes closed, he slid an iron band around his anger to control it as he listened to the conversation beyond this closed door.

Her description of their past together was cast with a very dingy lens. The facts were right, but the angle on which she told the story was all wrong.

His jaw hardened as she skewed things to make him look bad. She didn't have to do that. He had worked hard to maintain a certain image. And she was trashing it.

Nothing wrong with raw ambition.

He ground his teeth. So she wants her power back.

Not fucking going to happen.

Her power belonged to him. He owned it, like he owned her.

And he sure as fuck wasn't going to let her taint it, and herself, with that fucking dragon in there.

Conrad couldn't work with dragon magic. But he could do wonders with djinn magic. He'd already done much with what he'd siphoned from her all through those early years.

He was going to have to shore up the spell so that no one could break the bond, ever. He'd make sure once and for all that the lamp—and she—remained in his possession, where they belonged.

He just needed to think this through. He could do it, of course. But he'd need a plan; now that she was infatuated with that dragon, a new angle would be required.

Chapter Ten

B ayn and Gena took an extra day off work leading into the weekend. The two of them took their time traveling back, exploring wooded trails and visiting all the tourist sites they could manage along the way.

Neither of them had taken the time before.

Bayn realized how much he liked seeing the world from this perspective. It was a great way for Gena and him to get to know one another a little more. On the trails, she marveled at the budding trees, the song of the early-return birds, and the first bright green shoots emerging from the ground.

The museum sites were quaint. Hundred and fifty year old buildings, cherished by local humans, were but a blink to these two immortals, but it was easy to see what was valued. The everyday things preserved. Things and activities no one gives much thought to in the present, but set in the past told a story of how similar yet changed things were for their forebears.

Simple things. Human things.

While they were moving her bags into his townhouse from the car, he glanced at Gena. He hoped they could fix her magic problem before she permanently became human.

The last of the bags brought in and set in her room, he took her coat and put it away in the closet by the door.

"Why don't you use your magic for yourself?"

"I do. To teleport when I need to get somewhere."

"But you otherwise live as a human."

"Yes."

"Why?"

"I don't know. Maybe because I spent centuries as a magical being trapped in a lamp, I thought this would be a nice change. Live in the world like everyone else."

"You don't ever mingle with other paranormals?"

She shrugged.

"Well, we're going to be arranging public events. Galas to raise money for Elyssia's estate and collection. We'll be meeting a lot of potential patrons, among whom are old friends of mine that like to help out and get themselves some media time."

"Alright."

"We'll be meeting with the event planner Monday morning."

"You don't need me for that."

"I'd like you to be there for input. The more she knows about the project, the better, in terms of tone and expectation."

"You really are all-in, in the mortal world now, aren't you?" she said.

"Passes the time," He smiled at her. "Tea?" He moved into the kitchen to prepare the kettle.

"Yes, thanks. Tell me more about the goal of the project."

"Elyssia wanted to leave something behind of herself. She didn't have children, so she spent a lot of time out in her community working to make it better for everyone."

"Was she mortal?"

"A long-lived witch that loved her neighborhood. When I first came to the city, she invited me over, put me in contact with other paranormals in her network, and we stayed in touch since. She helped me establish my business."

"Fascinating. Do you see the others much?"

He shook his head. "Rarely. Cross paths on occasion, but it seems everyone is as busy as I am doing their thing."

She nodded. "Liv and I sometimes go years without contact, we both just get so busy. But other times, we're talking every other day. Weird."

He smiled and handed her a tea cup. "Just so you know, the planner is a paranormal too. And she has a larger than life personality. You'll like her."

"Witch? Shifter?"

"Wood nymph."

She laughed. "You're kidding!"

He sipped his tea. "Quinn recommended her."

"Small world. Seems everyone knows everyone. Except for me."

"Not everyone. I don't know this Conrad sorcerer you mentioned."

Her eyes snapped up to him from over the rim of her teacup. "When I knew him, he was very well known in our realm. Maybe he decided to step off the stage and into the shadows."

He nodded. Perhaps. He'd known a few sorcerers in his time. Either incredibly reclusive, working at things in the darkness, manipulating the world around them with an invisible hand, or standing in the open on display. Though less of the latter these days, with the world as it was. Most had taken that step back to avoid too much attention, which could hinder their machinations. Most paranormals remained hidden from the greater world.

When he looked at Gena again, her expression had changed. Eyes glued to his face.

"What is it?" he asked her.

She blinked. "You're the only dragon I've ever seen. I know almost nothing about you."

"These days, what you see is what you get."

"I'd love to see more of you." She laughed, a nervous sound, blushing. "I mean, see you in your dragon form again."

He leaned over the counter with a grin, "I'd love for you to see more of me too."

Her cheeks blazed and he chuckled.

"You should have mentioned that before we got back. We could have snuck out into a farmer's field and entertained ourselves with terrifying some cows."

Gena laughed. "Maybe, but I'd rather be entertained by terrifying someone that deserves it."

"I like your thinking. Like, maybe, some greedy magic thieves?"

"Maybe, like that." She smiled and sipped more of the tea. "I don't even know if he still lives."

"Conrad?"

She nodded. "I'm sure I wouldn't be sad if I never saw him again. But I wonder if he's the only one that can break the bond between me and the lamp."

Bayn straightened, putting his cup down. "There has to be a way that wouldn't involve him."

He reached for her hand, walked around the counter island to where she sat on the stool, and placed her palm against his chest. "In the meantime, why don't we go distract ourselves?" He raised a brow.

"Oh?" Her eyes searched his face, curiosity piqued.

He grinned, leaned forward and brushed his lips across hers. "Let's go for a little walk."

"Where are we going?" Gena asked again, unable to stop the giggle from escaping as Bayn led her along the now familiar downtown streets.

"You'll see," he said again.

By now, she recognized the street that led to his business building.

Work?

That's exactly where he led her. But instead of going to the office, the elevator took them further up.

He led her up to the roof of the skyscraper.

Her hand firmly in his, he opened the steel door and led her out onto the rooftop.

It was breathtaking.

The chilly spring winds curled around them, causing her hair to float about her head. It was a cloudless night with diamond stars winking overhead despite the city lights.

The view from their office windows was awesome, but this was spectacular—especially at night. Other skyscrapers loomed nearby, but most were dimly lit office buildings. The CN Tower was a beacon of color by the lake, and below them the streets were ribbons of white headlights and red taillights. Through the sounds of rooftop air filtration units, she could hear the distant chop of a traffic helicopter as it monitored the streets and highways.

Turning to Bayn, she said, "What are we doing up here?"

"You wanted to see my dragon. Short of taking an hour long drive out of the city, this is the best place to do that." He grinned. "Hopefully no one's paying attention to this roof." He nodded toward the buildings that rose above theirs.

"I could try to conjure an invisibility barrier," Gena said, holding up her hand.

Bayn put a hand over her fingers before she could snap them. "Conserve whatever you have. I've got this."

He smiled and stepped back a few paces. Eyes closed, he drew a deep breath. When he opened them again, they glowed that brilliant ice blue that she saw before when his magic flared against hers. He blew out his breath in a white cloud that billowed and grew, surrounding them. Inhale, exhale. The cloud of wispy fog and gathering ice crystals expanded to cover the perimeter of the rooftop and settled several feet above them.

It writhed all around them. A living thing made of his breath. The chill of it tickled her skin and whitened the outer threads of her hair.

She laughed, "This reminds me of the wonderland décor at Quinn's party." Her fingers wiggled through a curl of the mist floating past her.

He grinned at her with a wink as the blue of his eyes flared brighter. He began to change.

Her breath stalled in her chest as her eyes drank in the magnificence of his naked human form.

The air around him shimmered into a cloud similar to what floated around them, but was held together by the force of his magic.

It reminded her of her own black cloud when she shifted.

There was a surge of rainbow-like color swirling through the mist as it rearranged and changed form. Scales became visible as a haunch took shape. White claws curled and dug into the rooftop gravel.

She blinked, and the last of the opalescent cloud solidified.

A massive white dragon curled around her, his blue eyes trained on her face.

The cellophane-like membranes of his wings were folded down his back.

The primal part of her brain sent a shiver of awe through her body.

No matter that she too was ancient and powerful.

"You're so beautiful," she breathed, reaching out a hand to his snout. Her fingers slid along the smaller scales of his jaw, past the spikes that flared along it like glittering stalactites. "Never in all my years have I seen anything more so."

Her heart thumped.

The great beast that stood before her was overwhelming in beauty and power and awe. He could swallow her whole, extinguishing her life. Yet she knew he would never hurt her. She desperately wished she could climb atop his back and experience the skies as he did. But not tonight.

Laying her head against him, she closed her eyes and absorbed the moment, hands caressing him.

She stepped back, eyes open, unable to get enough of the magnificent sight.

"Exactly as I remembered." She smiled.

He pressed the tip of his snout to her chest. The blue of his eye flared as he inhaled deeply, the pupil narrowing.

The thud of the helicopter grew louder.

"I think it's coming this way." She laughed. "Probably to see the only cloud in the skies tonight, and see why it's floating over this building."

The dragon huffed and she stepped back from him with reluctance.

Again he was surrounded in a shimmering light as he returned to his human form. He grabbed her hand and pulled her back toward the door. With a last turn, his eyes flared and the magic holding the mist dissipated, allowing the filmy cloud to disperse.

The helicopter was indeed headed in their direction.

They quickly ducked through the door, abandoning the rooftop to the investigation of the inquisitive traffic helicopter pilot.

Gena's laughter echoed along the bare concrete walls of the hall, from the door back to the elevator.

They grinned at each other during the descent.

The doors slid open at the floor to their offices and Bayn unlocked the door. Leaving the lights off, they approached the windows and watched the helicopter circle the building, only able to imagine what the pilot and broadcaster were thinking.

After a few more minutes it veered away, the sound of its blades fading.

"I can't remember the last time I did anything that fun." she said.

He smiled at her, his fingers moving to fix some of the windblown strands of hair into place, tucking the last few behind her ear.

She glanced up at Bayn's hair, which was a wild mass of black waves standing up from his scalp. She reached up to let her fingers slide through it. A shiver rippled through her as she touched him. Stepping closer, she pressed her body to his, feeling his warmth seep through the layers of their clothing to warm her.

Capturing her hand, he trailed kisses from her palm to inner wrist, where the cuff of her jacket stopped his progress.

She'd never wanted her coat off faster than she did that moment, and with it all her clothes, so that he could plant kisses along whichever route he wanted to go on her skin.

Lifting his gaze to hers, his eyes were intensely dark on her face.

"I want you," she whispered.

The corner of his mouth lifted, "I know. I want you too."

She was breathless, staring at his lips.

I want you too.

Those words sent a flood of hot moisture down through her core. Her desire for him overwhelmed her, but it was more than just desire. Her heart hammered so hard in her chest it hurt.

Make love to me.

Love me.

As she stared into his eyes, there was no fear in her.

Reaching with hesitant fingers, she looked up into his face as her fingers slid his coat off his shoulders.

He made no move to stop her.

Hers dropped behind her.

Her fingers shook as she reached for the hem of his shirt next, sliding it up his taut abs. He raised his arms, dragging it the rest of the way over his head.

She licked her lips, staring at his bare chest and the intricately inked markings covering the sharp lines of his muscled torso.

Mouth watering, she stepped closer, inhaling deeply of his scent.

Power. Musk. Dragon.

Gena planted a soft kiss on the smooth skin over his beating heart, then worked her way down to his nipple.

He sucked his breath in with a hiss. Hands claiming her face, he drew her mouth toward his; his hot tongue swept her bottom lip.

Opening to him, he took her.

Her knees buckled and she fell against him with a moan.

Belt unbuckled, button and zipper rent, her nimble fingers sought his hard length.

Pressed to her palm, he throbbed.

Yes. He wanted her too.

Chapter Eleven

Bayn broke the kiss when Gena's soft fingers curled around his cock.

He swallowed a moan, and concentrated on breathing.

Breathing in her scent. The scent of her desire surrounded him. Called to him. His dragon was still close to the surface, urging him to claim her.

Not yet.

She must claim us first.

His dragon snorted his impatience.

Looking down into her upturned face, the city lights illuminated her with soft light. The office interior was otherwise dark.

Releasing him, she pushed her pants down from her hips. Then her panties.

Her blouse hung just below the shadow of her thigh, her secret world hidden from his view.

But he could smell her, igniting the memory of her taste.

He licked his lips, drawing her eyes to his mouth.

Her hand slid into the front of his jeans again, grasping him as she backed toward the tempered glass of the thick window pane, taking him with her.

There was nothing but city skyline behind her.

As clear as if they still stood atop the roof, or a cloud, for all he cared.

Back against the glass, she pulled him closer still, then pushed his jeans so they fell down around his knees. He kicked them off, freeing his legs.

Pressing his body to hers, he nestled between her moist thighs.

Mouths a breath apart, they took each other in.

Her knee slid up to his hip and her eyes opened into his.

"Please."

"You're sure?"

She nodded and lifted her mouth to his. Tongue to tongue.

He slid into her. She moaned and he almost came right then.

One hand held her ass so that her pelvis was hard against his, the other pressed splayed against the glass as he breathed to control himself.

Her tongue swept his mouth over and over, and her warm core gripped him so hot and tight, it took everything he had to hold back.

One moment, then two.

His breath shuddered with relief as he regained his control.

He opened his eyes. She stared back at him.

Tilting her hips, she gripped him tighter, sliding deeper.

He slid out to the tip, then slowly back in again.

Her eyes closed, letting her forehead fall into his shoulder.

"More."

Faster, deeper, harder.

She was like heaven. The sounds of her moans and gasps every time he slid home was all he wanted to hear for the rest of his long, long life.

She was his.

Mate.

She accepted him, but she hadn't claimed him yet. Not yet.

"Too much," she gasped, her eyes widening on his face as she came.

She was a hot, wet, velvety vice around his cock. An instant later, he surged into her. All that he was. Face buried in the hollow of her shoulder, curled around her, as she was curled around him. Pinned between his hips and the glass.

His fingers slid along the underside of her bottom until they found where they were intimately connected together. She shuddered.

"Don't go yet." She whispered.

"I'm not going anywhere, love."

Her eyes turned glassy and she quickly blinked away the emotion that flooded her face.

She tightened around him, eliciting a short groan from him. He hardened again almost immediately.

Unbuttoning the top of her blouse, she exposed her breast to him. Dipping his head, he licked and nibbled every exposed inch.

This time, when they loved again, it was much, much slower. Though just as explosive.

Walking back to Bayn's home, Gena stole glances, drinking in his profile under the city lights.

Her body sang. Her legs wobbled as they strolled along the streets.

She was all at once sated, yet hungry for more.

More of him.

Her very own aphrodisiac. A new drug.

The feel of him was intoxicating. The sound of his voice addictive. Especially when he moaned her name during their lovemaking. A breathy, low sound that thrummed through her most sensitive areas.

His fingers stroked hers as they walked, hand in hand. Like he was testing the reality of her existence.

He caught her looking at him and he grinned back at her.

She loved that boyish smile. The twinkle in his eye when he looked at her.

She loved the way he looked at her. Like *she* was precious.

Nothing like how others had looked at her lamp—at her power, and the possibilities.

She felt as though when he looked at her, she meant something to him.

Did she?

She wanted to.

She wanted to, because she realized she loved him. She always had. She'd buried it under the guise of infatuation at a distance. But her inner self knew.

A shiver rippled through her.

"Cold?" He asked, pulling her into the sphere of his embrace, his arm securely around her so she could lean into him.

Letting her head drop to his shoulder, she thought about what he'd done up there on the rooftop.

He'd let her see him. His true self. His power. All that he was.

Asking nothing in return.

He'd let her make the first moves. She'd taken him in.

What would she give back to him?

What did he want? If anything?

She wouldn't ask. Not right now. Maybe later, when they settled in, back at his home over a cup of hot tea.

Right now, she wanted to bask in the magic of their lovemaking.

That was true magic.

C onrad crackled.

His anger surrounded him, extending from the malicious, vengeful thoughts that permeated his body.

He'd followed his djinn and the dragon from his home. Listened in on their mundane chatter. Listened in on the rooftop sounds, following where he could without detection.

He'd listened.

He listened through the sounds of their fucking. Hating that those same sounds had him hard and ready. Alone and unsated. And they'd fucked again. The second time, he jerked himself off as he listened, to ease the frustration. Imagining her lithe body. He'd been her first, all those years ago.

She let the dragon touch her.

This wouldn't do.

He had to take her back. Now. Before it was too late. Before the dragon had dominance over her and Conrad couldn't reach her again.

Chapter Twelve

Gena had taken to carrying her lamp with her everywhere she went, rather than leave it behind at Bayn's house.

They were working closely with Marisole, the planner, to get the finishing touches ready for the Gala.

Elyssia's artifacts had been brought into the office to choose which would dazzle attendees the most, and inspire the highest bids.

After weeks of intense work researching the items for this project, a couple dozen had been chosen for the showcase. Her work wasn't anywhere near finished, but this was a stepping stone in the project, to raise its profile and bring in funding for the estate curation.

"As soon we have our choices made, I can take the profiles you wrote up with the pictures to the printer and get the Gala's guide done," Bayn said, arms crossed as he surveyed the room full of shiny objects.

"That grouping over there, for sure," Marisole said, scribbling notes on her clipboard. "This lot, I'm not so sure. They're not as spectacular. More valuable, yes. But fancy, no."

Reaching for the purse she'd left on the floor between the cabinet and her desk, Gena extracted a pen. "I'll record the catalog numbers of the ones you've chosen, then pack them up till shipping time." Gena said, stepping away from the corner of the room she'd been occupying all morning.

"Perfect. Oh, what's this?" Marisole bent to retrieve something at floor level.

When she stood, Gena could feel the blood drain from her face.

"Now this is exquisite. Why haven't I seen it before? It should be the jewel of the gala," she breathed.

Bayn stepped forward, gently lifting Gena's lamp from Marisole's splayed hands. Eyes round, she didn't object to the loss, but the question remained on her face. "It's not part of

Elyssia's collection," he said, handing the gilded lamp back to Gena.

Gena quickly stuffed it back in her bag and pulled the zipper closed.

Careless.

Her hands shook with the shock of seeing it in someone else's hands. After several deep breaths, the panic buzzing in her head eased, and she realized that Marisole didn't seem to show any signs of the intense covetousness that she usually saw in beholders.

"Are you sure? It looks like the sort of thing Elyssia would have stuck a strawberry plant in. That piece could potentially finance the whole estate project."

"I'm sure," Gena said, relaxing a fraction. "It's an heirloom."

Up until that very moment, no one other than Liv and Bayn had seen the lamp since before it landed in his lair, let alone touched it.

Marisole shrugged and turned her attention back to the remaining artifacts up for decision.

As she leaned over the table, Bayn mouthed 'Wood Nymph' over her head to Gena.

Smiling, Gena realized that he'd told her that Marisole was a wood nymph when he mentioned they'd be working with her on the Gala.

The fern in the corner of her office was in more danger of being lifted than the solid gold, centuries-old jewel encrusted lamp stashed in her purse.

The sky was black beyond the office windows by the time they made their decisions and had them packed for eventual transportation. It wouldn't be long now. Bayn would put a rush order on the print copies of the guide, to be distributed the night of the Gala.

Marisole bid them all good night. Kaylie made the round of the offices, locking things up and turning off excess lights.

"We'll get the rest," Bayn said, "See you in the morning."

"G'night boss." She smiled and waved at Gena through the glass wall and slipped out the door.

"I can't believe how smoothly everything is going," Gena said as she switched off her own office lights and picked up her jacket and purse. Waiting for Bayn to finish up what he was doing, she set her purse on Kaylie's desk and slung her jacket around her shoulders. "I'll be glad when it's warm enough I don't need this thing," she said, dropping her hands into her pockets out of habit. Her fingers slipped over the dime she kept forgetting was there. She couldn't even remember why it was in her pocket and not her purse in the first place.

With a glance at Bayn, she fished her change purse out of her larger bag and dropped the coin into it, then dropped the little change purse back into the bag, settling it into the compartment beside the lamp. She secured the zipper and slung the bag up onto her shoulder as he emerged from his darkened office.

"Grocery shopping?"

"Only if there are sweet buns and black sesame paste on the list." She grinned mischievously at him.

"You got it." He pulled her in close to steal a soft kiss.

Dumping the bags on the counter, Bayn said, "I'm wondering if there's a new paranormal in town. Every now and then, for the last few weeks, I feel a brush of muted power nearby that I can't pinpoint."

Gena turned to him, eyebrow raised. "Good or bad?"

He shrugged and opened a cupboard door. "Can't tell, honestly. Like I said, they keep their magic muted."

"Speaking of magic, any word from Liv or Quinn? It's been ages."

"No," he said, and thought a few moments. "I'll give her a call though. She wouldn't have forgotten, but she seems to always have something going on."

Gena nodded. "Thanks. I'll call Liv, too," she said, and took her purse off into the bedroom he'd given her, though she hadn't slept in it much the last while.

He grinned. What little sleep they did get was usually elsewhere; in his bed, on the couch, floor, bathtub. Wherever they fell, exhausted, that wasn't too uncomfortable.

She still hadn't claimed him.

And he wouldn't push.

But he could sense there was something that hung between them. A question she wouldn't ask.

Her face was an open book. She'd nearly let it out several times now, but swallowed it back down.

Disappointed, he let it slide.

She would ask when she was ready.

And he understood that question needed to be asked and answered before she could think about claiming him.

He had all the time in the world.

Did she?

They still hadn't sorted out the problem with her magic. And she hadn't dared try to use it in case it depleted further, without knowing the consequences if that happened.

Fear slithered up his spine.

If she lost her power and turned mortal, he couldn't be sure how his dragon magic would affect her, in combination with her djinn magic. He could lose her within less than a century. The thought was unbearable.

He swallowed the heartache that threatened to choke him. He drew a breath.

If that were the case, if she turned permanently mortal, then he would have to make the most of the time they did have together.

Cherish her—like no other treasure he'd had before.

Pulling his cell from his pocket, he called Quinn.

"Bayn! I'm so sorry I haven't got back to you before now. I've got a couple of names for you, but I haven't been able to verify them myself before passing them along. Sorcerers don't live out in the open like they used to, and djinns are generally even more elusive."

"Not a problem, Quinn. Thanks for taking the time."

"I'll text you what I have. But I really can't vouch for any of them."

"Understood."

"Take care, and good luck."

Her words were laced with concern.

Proceed with extreme caution.

He leaned a hip against the counter island as he waited for her message to ping through. Seconds later, he thumbed the names. There were just a handful.

Five. Three had sad face emojis next to them, the other two had question marks.

Not great.

He glanced down the hall toward the open door to the room Gena was in, talking to Olivia. The sound of her laugh carried back down the hall to him in the kitchen.

He smiled.

Placing the phone back in his pocket, he considered how to go about this. The remaining names had general city locations, none of which were within their current country borders. No phone numbers attached. If it were known, Quinn would have provided it.

So that meant traveling. They only had a few days before the Gala. Gena couldn't teleport and she wouldn't leave the lamp behind. Trying to travel traditionally with it on short notice would be a customs nightmare.

He could wait until after the Gala. Or he could just take care of it before the big night. He could go alone and check out these sorcerers for himself. Unease settled in his gut.

There was a new paranormal lurking in the neighborhood that he hadn't sniffed out yet. Would she be safe on her own? Was there any reason to think she wouldn't be?

He wouldn't have thought so, were it not for the fact she was inseparable from the thing.

She would be a wreck of anxiety if he talked her into leaving it locked away somewhere during the Gala, if she didn't talk him into letting her carry the thing all night.

She seemed to be becoming much more at ease with him, but in all other respects, when it came to the lamp, her hyper-awareness seemed to be increasing. He didn't like seeing her so ill at ease. He was beginning to really, really resent the power the thing held over her. How could she have lived like this for so long?

Then he remembered. She'd pretty much lived like a hermit, never straying far or for long. The proxy of a controlling spouse.

He needed to help her gain the total freedom Olivia had wished for her.

They needed help.

Chapter Thirteen

Gena sensed Bayn's absence before she fully awakened.

Alone in the bed, she rolled over and sat up to listen for him elsewhere in the house.

Not a sound.

"Bayn?"

Rising from the bed, she reached for her thin wrap, pulling the edges tight to her torso. She peeked into the ensuite, knowing it was empty, then padded down the stairs toward the kitchen and living room, which were also empty.

This was the third night she'd awakened alone.

Where had he gone?

By the time the morning alarm went off, he was usually back in the bed, body curled around hers.

Maybe he went to check his treasure hoard?

These last few nights were the first time since she'd moved into his house that he'd begun disappearing in the wee hours of the night.

Old habits?

Pouring herself a glass of milk, she considered the lamp stashed in her purse.

Still.

She had no grounds to grumble if he still had his issues. She sure still had hers.

Wandering toward where the purse sat, she glared at it.

She hated it. She hated how attached to it she was.

The more she let herself fall into the relationship with Bayn, the heavier the weight of lamp became, always keeping that much distance between them.

She loved him. She wanted him. She wanted him for always. And she could sense he might want that too.

She'd looked up often enough to catch him, staring at her unguardedly. His attention was a tether, but the lamp pulled her back again. She strained between the two grounding points.

His patience was constant. For now. How long could he maintain it? How long before he realized she didn't know how to let go of the lamp and embrace him wholly?

Until then, she could not commit to him. She could not hope that he would claim her and she could not think about claiming him in return.

How long before they could find a sorcerer that could advise her how to break away from the lamp?

He deserved better. He deserved someone that would commit to him.

Not what she was doing. It was unfair.

Maybe that's why he'd gone back to the familiarity of his treasure hoard. She was no longer holding that interest for him.

I should go home.

The thought settled with the weight of iron slag in the pit of her stomach.

In all these weeks with him, he'd cared for her, and she still had not given anything of herself in return.

She couldn't.

She wasn't sure she could, even if the issue with the lamp and her power were resolved once and for all.

As much as she wanted to be with him, she feared she could never be all that he deserved.

And a life time of that—especially an immortal lifetime of that—was a very long time.

It wasn't that she feared he was like Conrad, or that he'd ever be anything like him.

She feared that Conrad had damaged her beyond repair. His deeds would forever be a shadow over her life. The lamp was a constant reminder of that betrayal and abuse.

And she could not let it go. It was part of her. Enmeshed into her core identity. She was the lamp and the lamp was her.

She sniffled and drew a deep breath, noticing the wetness of tears dripping from her cheeks. Swiping a hand across her face, she went in search of a tissue to blow her nose. Re-entering the master bedroom, she stumbled to a stop.

Bayn stood in the middle of the room looking at the empty bed.

"Gena? What's wrong?" He stepped toward her, his boots soundless on the carpet.

She sniffled, turned toward the bathroom and returned with the needed tissue, her eyes on his face.

He smelled of the cool outside night air.

Face clean, the tissue crumbled into a little ball in her fist. "I think, after the Gala, I'll head back home to Ottawa. Most of the research work is done for what you need. The rest I can do remotely."

His brows went up, his lips parted as he sucked in a breath. "Why?"

Her heart crumbled a little, seeing the shocked disappointment on his handsome face. Standing as he was, hair tousled, collar open, pulse ticking at his throat, she wanted nothing more than to slide her hands between the cool leather jacket and his warm skin. To kiss his pulse point to ease his confusion. To feel his arms slide around her and take her back to the empty bed.

Her eyes slid to its expanse. Rumpled sheets and duvet thrown aside.

Welcoming.

Misleading?

That space, where they made love, wove a magic of illusion.

An illusion of a relationship she desperately wanted, but could not reach out and claim.

"We'll talk in the morning," she said, voice tight as she slipped out of the room, toward the room she'd originally intended to sleep in all this time.

"Gena?"

His fingers touched hers as she stepped into the hall.

A gentle brush that made the last few feet to the other room feel like he held her fast, reeling her backward the further she stepped.

"Good night, Bayn."

She didn't look at him as she took the last step into the vacant room with the alien bed that did not smell anything like him.

Bayn didn't return to the empty bed after he watched Gena leave his room.

He could see right away something had changed, in the way she refused to meet his eyes.

Was she upset to wake alone? Was she frightened?

No, he didn't think that was it. Something else.

She clearly wasn't going to tell him, as much as he wanted to force her to utter the words.

He swallowed the emotions roiling through his chest.

Unease. Not right. Upset.

His dragon muttered these concepts.

Claim.

Can't.

His response was met with a snarl.

Ignoring it, he stripped and showered to try to think straight.

His body sagged under the hot water, bracing his hands on the wall, he let it fall over his head.

He sought the patience to accept the space she still needed. To not go and take what he wanted and claim her as his own, like his instinct instructed him to do.

He'd told her he wanted her.

She'd said she wanted him too.

He drew a deep breath.

Fucking lamp.

He needed to figure out how to help her. He'd spent the last few nights seeking out the last couple of sorcerers on the list. Trying to pinpoint their location so he could talk to them directly.

He was a dragon, their magic was useless against him, but he needed to keep as much distance between them and Gena as possible until he could determine their nature. Which he couldn't do until he found the fuckers.

His teeth ground in frustration and fatigue.

He'd even sought out one of the sad face emoji sorcerers.

And quickly understood why Quinn had tagged them with that particular emoji.

Bitter old bastard.

His aura oozed fuckery. No way he was going to drop even the slightest hint that he knew a djinn, let alone had one holed up at his house.

His fist curled and wavered.

He resisted the urge to throw his fist through the shower tiles in a tantrum, and instead pressed his open palm against it, seeking a sense of grounding.

Chapter Fourteen

A knock on the front door pulled Bayn's attention from his coffee pot.

He opened it to find Olivia's bright blue eyes staring up at him with concern. "You look like crap."

"Hey Liv, good to see you. How'd you know where I live?" he said, his voice flat.

"Gena."

"Of course." He stepped aside to grant her entrance.

Shucking her coat off, she opened the hall closet in front of her and hung it up. "You should sleep," she said, slipping her feet out of her shoes. "I'm going to talk to Gena." She wandered through the house, looking left and right till she found the stairs.

Bayn sighed, closed the door and shuffled back to his coffee pot, with a solemn glance up the stairs. His keen hearing picked up the sounds of Gena and Olivia talking in her room at the end of the hall.

Olivia's voice rose.

He glanced at his watch.

He had to go.

Marisole needed him to sign off on the final touches for this evening's event.

He'd hoped Gena would have seen the project through to the end with him.

Claim her, idiot.

Shut up. He snarled back at his dragon.

She's our treasure.

She's her own person that has to make her own decisions. And she hasn't chosen us.

Yet.

Not yet. He agreed. *I know she wants to.*

Bayn's dragon snorted. *Obviously.*

Go back to sleep.

Can't. Treasure. Mate.

Bayn rolled his eyes and sipped his black coffee.

Can't force her.

Not like the old days.

Nope.

Bayn sighed, finished his coffee, and went to rinse his cup in the sink. Setting it aside, he cast a last glance up the stairs and made his way out the door. He hoped the walk to the office would help clear some of the melancholy from his heart.

"What the frig do you mean, you're going home?" Liv's voice rose an octave.

Gena glanced at the closed bedroom door.

"Anyone with a brain in their head can see that man adores you, Gena."

"That's beside the point. If you can't take me back, I'll book a train."

"You're not taking the train anywhere, and I sure as hell am not going to take you back. You're being ridiculous."

"What are you so upset about? This has nothing to do with you." Gena snapped.

Gena and Olivia had never—*ever*—argued before. Especially not with raised voices.

Nor could she recall the last time she'd heard Olivia curse like that.

"This has everything to do with me. I frigged up the wish that was supposed to free you. *I* frigged it up somehow, and all these years—these last few centuries—you've been living like you're still trapped inside the damned *thing*."

Gena bit her lip as Olivia's words struck her like slaps the face and a kick to the gut.

She kept going.

"He's your mate. Your *Mate*. I know it. And I know *you* know it too. So what the hell, Gena?"

Liv's anger rolled toward Gena in hot waves. Face red, she stood with feet splayed and fists on hips. Her blue eyes narrowed on her.

Gena looked away, dropping her gaze to her hands resting on her lap.

"Gena! You're a frikking djinn. Look at me! You're one of the most powerful beings in this world, and you're sitting there like a scared rabbit while I yell at you. You have the power to think me out of existence, and look at you."

She drew in a shuddering breath.

Olivia blew out a sigh and dropped onto the edge of the bed next to her.

"I love you Gena, but I can't let you throw this away. We'll figure this out together." She grasped Gena's hand in hers and squeezed it.

They both heard the front door click shut, followed by the sound of Bayn's boots treading across the front porch and down the steps.

Gena sagged.

Olivia was quiet a long time before she spoke again, her voice soft. "Nick has seen an awful lot of kids that have seen too much and experienced more than anyone ever should. He's told me, more than once, that you remind him of those kids he's seen." She squeezed her hand again. "Some of them do find happiness. The ones that rise above the crappiness they've been dealt. They struggle, but they do achieve it. And they're just humans. They don't have the power that you do."

"What does it matter that I'm supposed to have power if I'm broken?"

"Maybe it doesn't." Olivia shrugged. "But, nor do you need to be broken, either."

Gena stared at her bag, set next to the bedroom door. The morning light filtered in through the window, making the small bit of exposed gold on the lamp gleam.

"How do they do it?"

"Nick said he thinks they just decide to accept what was. Embrace it as part of them, and move on, despite the fear."

"He makes it sound easy."

"He's never said he thought it was. Those few that succeed, rarely have done it alone. They've all found someone that supports them. A lover, a friend, a mentor, another family member."

Gena lifted her eyes to Olivia's.

Tears streamed down her friend's face. "I'm here. *He*'s here for you too."

"I don't know how. That's the problem."

Liv nodded. "I've been thinking about that. I know everything in you resists the idea of destroying the lamp."

Gena sucked in a deep breath, her spine snapping upright at the mention of it.

"See? I get that's not okay, so we don't do that. What if we do something else?"

"Like?"

"Change it. Change it so it's not a lamp that can trap you anymore. Melt it down, shape it into something else. Something of your choosing. You control what shape it takes."

Gena's gut didn't buck at the idea. Maybe she could consider that.

"A different shape."

"Yeah, like maybe a shield, or a sword, something to protect you instead of threaten you."

Gena laughed, "I can't walk the city streets with a gold sword or shield; that would be ridiculous."

Olivia's smile was gentle. "It would. But it'd be yours." She shrugged.

Mine. Take it back.

"It was mine to begin with. A gift from my father," she said, her voice faint. "It just happened to be the nearest durable vessel in the room when Conrad performed the spell. He twisted it."

Olivia didn't respond.

"It's been through a lot, and never been tarnished, scratched or dented. I wouldn't know where to start."

"I bet I know a dragon with powerful magic that could probably help with that." Olivia grinned, bumping her shoulder against Gena's.

The bitch is crazy!

Conrad paced as he listened to Gena whine about her situation to her friend.

He could not believe she was actually considering melting down the lamp and turning it into something else.

What a stupid idea.

Doubt wriggled at the base of his skull.

What if it worked? What if by doing this, transforming it, she could break the bond permanently?

If that were the case, he'd better move his ass and get it back before she had time to do anything stupid or think of more idiotic ideas concerning the lamp.

Chapter Fifteen

B ayn looked up at his office door as it
swished open to reveal Gena.

Expression uncertain, she stepped in and
closed the door behind her.

They stared at one another a long moment.

"I've been trying to-"

"I want to ask you-"

"Go ahead," Bayn said. He drew a deep breath
as she stepped forward. "What do you want to
ask me?"

"It was Liv's idea. Can you help me change the
lamp—if it can be done?"

"Of course." He blew out the breath he'd been
holding, then smiled. He moved around from
behind the desk toward her. Reaching for her,
he slid his hands up her arms, over her shoul-

ders and cupped her face. "I've been trying to track down sorcerers for information."

"That's where you've been going?"

He nodded.

"Why didn't you tell me?"

"In case I couldn't find one that would help. Quinn gave me some names and rough locations, but they're bloody hard to find."

Gena nodded.

"How do you want to change the lamp?"

Her slim shoulders shrugged under his hands. "I'm not sure. Liv suggested your dragon magic could do it."

"Okay. What do you want to change it into?"

"I don't know yet, but the idea is that hopefully, your dragon magic will break Conrad's spell. I know that whatever shape we make it, it isn't another vessel of sorts. Something solid. Maybe an amulet, or a bracelet that I can wear."

Bayn nodded.

"I've never come across other djinn artifacts in my time. I was young when I was entrapped."

"We'll figure it out." He kissed the space between her brows.

"Thank you." She looked up at him with her liquid dark eyes. "For now, we should get to work on the Gala."

"Okay." He smiled. The tension in his chest eased. She wasn't leaving.

He drew in a deep breath and pulled her into his arms, and was relieved when hers slid round his waist.

They both exhaled, their bodies pressed closer so that they could feel the beat of the other's heart.

Perfect.

The night of the Gala.

Gena leaned closer to the mirror to apply the black eyeliner and shadow to her eyes. She didn't need mascara, her lashes were naturally black and thick. If she were a vain woman, she'd say her eyes were her best feature.

She stared at herself in the mirror.

Normally, she'd do what she had to and move away from it as quickly as possible. But lately, the happier she felt, the more emboldened she was to stare just a little longer.

She looked, until she saw only her eyes.

The 'windows to the soul' they say.

She could see a glimmer of something in the reflection of her irises.

She blinked, but resisted the reflex to look away.

Instead she leaned closer. Looked deeper.

"I see you in there." She whispered to herself. A pang of deep truth struck her heart. The shape of a flame formed in the reflection. Smokeless flame. The legends of the birth of a djinn. The source of her power. Her power was a flame, buried at her core.

I am the vessel of my power.

She blinked again. Where had that come from?

What did it mean? She glanced at the reflection of her lamp in the background behind her.

I am my vessel.

She thought of Bayn. He didn't question his power. He *was* his power.

Gena vaguely recalled the days before her entrapment.

The days before the doubt. The days before she gave her power away to a man she loved, who used it to enslave her to his whims.

She'd lost who she was centuries ago. Or so she had thought, as she stared more deliberately into the mirror.

No. Gena the djinn was still there. Waiting. Waiting for her to complete the process of re-claiming her freedom. Her power. Herself.

She gasped as the black of her iris slid out to coat the whites of her eyes so they were completely in liquid shadow.

Free us.

A flame burned in her chest like nothing she'd felt before.

The surge of her power threatening to over-whelm her body frightened her and she backed away from the mirror in fear as she struggled to control what she had long suppressed.

The rage.

She swallowed it down. Clamped down hard.

She would not let it out.

Gena feared she would lose control of it—herself—and become a weapon of destruction, if she unleashed her true power. She could not lose control.

That was her greatest fear.

She'd become so broken, she did not trust that she wouldn't use her power to destroy, should her rage become uncontrollable.

Conrad used to warn her that her power needed to be contained and controlled. She was a potential danger to others.

If she did let it out, would it burst en masse, then burn out?

Would it take her, and everyone around her, with it?

Did she even have enough power left in her to do anything at all? Maybe it was all just fear.

Something was going on with her magic and she had no idea what.

First it was fading—draining.

Now, suddenly it's struggling to burst forth.

Maybe it was her extended proximity to Bayn?

They'd thought to look for other sorcerers to break the final link of Conrad's spell. Maybe she should be looking for other djinn.

Her mother had left her to her own devices after her father had died.

He'd tried to warn her away from the human sorcerer Conrad.

She hadn't listened. She'd followed her heart. Lost it, and her family, and herself, in the process.

Family.

She'd stopped thinking about them centuries ago. Gena didn't even know if her mother ever tried to find her. She doubted it. They weren't like human families. But she did have such fond memories of her father.

Her eyes landed on the lamp. A gift.

A human metallurgist. Goldsmith. He'd made the lamp. A gift of light. Meant to hold oil to fuel a flame to hold darkness at bay.

He'd told her she was his little flame.

Her father was the light of her life, while she had him. He died after she had found Conrad, and her mother had had little interest in her. Not even to teach her about her power.

That, she'd learned the hard way.

A fit of temper had resulted in the loss of several innocent lives. Her mother had smirked. "You're too much like your father. Too much empathy."

Like it was a bad thing.

Anger flared in her chest, surprising her after being buried for so long.

Gena blinked away the ancient memories. There was no time to lose herself in the past. She drew a deep breath and squared her shoulders.

There was work to do.

A Gala. A tremor of fear rippled through her. People. Lots of unknown people.

I can do this. For Bayn.

The fear didn't ease, but she took one step, then another. On her way by the lamp, she scooped it up and dropped it into her bag, then went down to meet Bayn by the door.

It was time.

C onrad pulled at the collar of his suit.

His neck itched.

He huffed as he snatched another glass of champagne from the server that passed his post, standing by the third pillar down the long room, which was quickly filling with wealthy guests.

He leaned from one foot to the other, craning to see across the coiffed heads.

Where is she?

He knocked the champagne back, and left his glass by a planter before wandering to inspect the gleaming items in the display cases strategically placed throughout the room.

Gaudy.

Plain.

Cracked.

Too much patina.

Even more gaudy than the first.

He leaned away from the pristine glass, mouth twisted. His eyes swept the crowd again.

Stunning.

He made a noise of disgust as the dragon appeared next to her, taking her hand to guide her about the room toward a particular cluster of guests. The dragon's head lifted as his gaze swept the room in Conrad's direction.

His vision phased as he did a quick mental check of his magic shield.

The dragon's attention moved on.

Conrad moved along, angling himself so that he stayed out of both Gena's and the dragon's lines of sight.

He wasn't ready to let her see him yet.

Chapter Sixteen

D espite all her anxiety before the big event, Gena was actually beginning to enjoy the evening.

Bayn had been her dutiful escort; at her side from the moment they left the house until he had to step up to the podium to make his gala speech, to speak of his friend Elyssia and her mission to create the local museum. Expressing why he needed everyone's help to successfully complete this task in her name.

He was an eloquent speaker, as at ease before a crowd as he was when alone.

Gena wished she had such confidence and ease in her own skin.

Much like Quinn's Christmas party, where they'd been reunited, Bayn had taken Gena's hand and toured her around the room to meet and chat with the guests.

She'd been surprised to find herself actually enjoying the interactions, when she realized she was no longer seeing the gala as a crowd of strangers, but as meeting a series of small groups of people interested in their work.

However, there'd been a sense of unease in the pit of her gut that had nothing to do with her anxiety over a crowded space of strangers.

When they had approached the front of the room where the podium stood, Gena remained in the background, close to an open door that led to the corridor, hands clasped behind her back.

Bayn smiled and kissed her. "Wish me luck."

"Always."

She thought she'd seen Conrad—or someone that looked remarkably like Conrad—among the unknown faces just as Bayn stepped away to make his speech.

Her body went cold. She blinked.

The man stood staring directly at her, part way down the room, leaning on a pillar.

It couldn't really be him, could it?

His mouth curled at the corners and her stomach rolled over.

Oh. No.

His head turned as he looked at Bayn, who was still speaking and charming the crowd.

What does he want?

How did he find me?

Her breath came in gasps, her gaze shooting to Bayn.

Would Conrad do something to jeopardize that gala? She and Bayn, along with Marisole, had worked so hard to make this night as perfect as possible.

The lamp!

What other reason could he be here for?

She stood frozen, staring at him. She could no longer hear Bayn's speech over the hammering of her heart.

Did she have enough magic to do something?

In front of all of these human guests? No, not that.

Would *he* use magic in such a public place?

She'd left the lamp locked in Bayn's office safe, with a light dusting of magical warding around it and the office in general.

She still didn't know why her magic wasn't returning, and couldn't be sure how much she had left.

Her stomach flipped, unsure if she could defend herself from Conrad.

She glanced around the room, considering her options.

She stepped closer to the open door next to her.

Conrad's head turned back toward her, drawn by her movement.

Hands still behind her back, she drew her fingertips together trying to build a small flame of magic. As soon as there was enough gathered, she snapped her fingers.

The room instantly froze.

It wouldn't hold long, but long enough.

She stepped into the hall and let herself dissolve into the black mist of her essence. Struggling to control the weakened magic, she mentally threw herself into Bayn's office, where she reappeared and her molecules snapped back together painfully.

Gena dropped to the floor, panting.

She prayed the warding was strong enough he couldn't detect where she'd gone.

Staggering to her feet, she drew in a steadying breath.

Think.

Would she have been safer at the gathering?

Fuck.

Her panic drove her to try to protect the lamp.

As long as the wards held, he couldn't know where she was. But how had he found her in the first place? Her thoughts cascaded, ramping up her fear. She closed her eyes and drew in a deep breath, then walked toward the safe. Punching in the code, the door clicked open to reveal the gold and jewels gleaming in the dim evening light that filtered in through the windows. She closed it again, hand resting on the door.

A soft click drew her attention to the outer room, visible through the glass wall dividing the office space from Kaylie's reception desk.

Bayn?

Heart in her throat, she stepped out to meet him. By the time she reached Kaylie's desk, the door had eased open to reveal a back-lit male figure with a halo of blond hair illuminated by the golden hall lights.

She stepped back, bumping into the solid desk.

Conrad.

Conrad dropped the lock picks into the pocket of his tuxedo.

The door had been warded against magical tampering. He could have spent the time trying to overpower it, but it was faster just to pick the lock and save his energy.

He was pretty sure she had fled to the office—it was the closest escape and he knew he'd have to act fast. Surely the dragon would notice her absence in no time.

He released the handle, and the door swung inward. She stood in the middle of the reception area, her silhouette back-lit by the cityscape beyond the floor to ceiling windows of the offices.

Finally.

"It's been a long time, Gena."

"Not long enough."

He smiled at the tremble in her voice. "Awe, that isn't nice now, is it?"

She didn't answer him.

He sighed. "Just tell me where it is, and we can get on with the inevitable."

"No."

Conrad snorted at her defiance as he reached over to switch on the office light. He wanted to see her beauty up close.

She blinked at the sudden brightness, head turned away from it.

He approached her, but she didn't move from her position backed against the reception desk. Placing a finger under her chin, he forced her to look at him.

Liquid dark eyes framed in long black lashes glared up at him.

She'd looked at him with adoration, long ago. Before he decided to solidify the bond to make her his servant.

He shrugged. His property. His right to do as he pleased.

He passed his other hand, palm inches from her forehead. "Your magic is weak." He tsked. "You've been using it for yourself, haven't you?"

Gena shoved his hands away from her face. "Don't touch me."

Conrad snatched her wrist up, gripping it hard, "I'll do as I please. And you'll do as you're told. Now give me my lamp."

"No."

He twisted. Ignoring her cry of pain, he dragged her into the office she'd emerged from. "I know the safe is in here and you probably put it in there for tonight. I haven't seen you without it, otherwise."

"You've been watching me?"

"Of course I have. Now open the safe."

"Or what?" she spat at him.

She'd grown feisty.

"Any number of things," he growled, pulling her hard against him. "I am your master and I control your power—I control *you*." He looked down into her face, now full of rage. There were twin flames in her black irises. He chuckled. "I know you're fucking that lizard downstairs and I also know you have a human friend. A human friend that's vulnerable to magic. And I have quite the imagination."

She gasped.

He grinned.

"That's your problem, Gena. You've always been too damned soft. You make it so easy for me to do anything I please, no matter your protests. You always give in. Now give me my lamp." He shoved her toward the safe.

She glanced toward the door to the office suite.

He turned in time to see the lizard in question fill the door frame.

Flicking his hand toward it, his magic sent the door slamming closed. With a swirl of his fingers and a few muttered words, he cast a barrier spell.

The dragon hammered the door calling her name.

"Your magic isn't strong enough against a dragon's."

"No, but it's strong enough to keep him from coming through that door." He moved so that he was inches from her, next to the closed safe. "While the majority of your magic is bound to the function of the lamp, I've been siphoning your magic every time you used it for your own purposes. And I can tell that lately, you've been using it more than usual." He rolled his shoulders, straightening his spine so that he towered over her. Intimidating her.

The hammering on the door continued another moment.

"Bastard. If I could wish anything for myself it would be to be free of you," she snarled at him.

He smirked at her. "The lamp, Gena. If you don't give it to me now, I'll take out my frustrations on your friend until you submit. I don't care how long it takes, I'll live forever, remember?"

"I remember." Her beautiful face became stony.

"Good." He shoved her against the safe. "You, or your friend."

Pressing the buttons in sequence, the safe door swung open to reveal the item he'd been seeking for centuries.

The unnatural gleam of the gold and jewels drew his attention. He stood transfixed.

The desire to possess was overwhelming. He reached for it, needing to have it in his hands.

By the time he noticed the gathering fog growing enough to obscure the large office windows, it was too late.

A massive silver-gray tail materialized out of the fog, whipping toward the glass. It exploded from the force, shards flying in all directions.

Gena had dropped to a crouch, hands covering her head.

Before Conrad had the chance to shake his stupor, a claw also materialized from the glittering fog filtering into the room. It reached in, curling around Gena, and pulled her out of the office.

She vanished into the cloud.

The tail dissipated as the fog swirled and writhed upward.

Conrad grabbed the lamp and commanded Gena's return.

Nothing happened.

That fucking dragon's magic was blocking him!

How long could he hold that form? Indefinitely?

He'd seen the reports of weird sightings atop this building recently and recalled the events of the night he'd eavesdropped on the djinn and the dragon up there.

Conrad ran for the roof, lamp in hand.

Chapter Seventeen

B ayn lowered his fist from the door.

Gena was in trouble and the door was magically barricaded against him.

He needed to find another way to her. He ran for the elevator to the roof.

As soon as he stepped out into the open space he dematerialized into a state of mist, and went over the side of the building toward his office window.

He was mindful that it was another clear night and the sight of fog spilling over the edge of a high-rise might be noticed. As he reached the right floor, he hovered, observing. It only took seconds to see the man physically handling Gena toward the safe in his office and the strained expression on her face as she keyed in the code.

The intruder stood transfixed, staring at the safe.

Bayn needed to get Gena to safety. Fast.

With a whip of his substantial tail, and a swipe of his claw, he had her and was retreating up the building back toward the roof where he deposited her safely on her feet.

Some cloud matter remained as Bayn rematerialized in his human form. "Who the hell is that?"

"Conrad."

"Fuck."

His mind raced.

The door to the rooftop banged open.

Bayn stepped between Gena and the door as Conrad emerged, lamp in hand.

"He's strong, Bayn. My magic is weak because he's been siphoning it."

Thief. Bayn's dragon snarled.

"All of it?"

Bayn's dragon magic was over-matched for a sorcerer, but a sorcerer pumped up with powerful djinn magic? He couldn't be sure.

We should have claimed her.

Not helpful right now. Bayn told his dragon as he growled.

Crush the lamp.

Can't.

"I don't know," Gena replied.

Conrad approached, lamp raised.

Bayn dissolved and enveloped Gena against whatever spell Conrad was about the cast.

"You can't stay like that forever, lizard."

Lizard?

Gena raised her fingers, a flame flared to life.

"Go ahead, use it." Conrad smirked.

She extinguished the flame immediately.

That damned lamp was going to be their destruction.

Conrad stood before them, lamp handle clenched in his fist. It seemed to flare with a light of its own in the dull light of the night sky. Gena's life force was bound to that object.

He wished he could think of how to sever the link.

The irony didn't escape him.

He'd never wished for anything in his life. Just taken what he'd wanted.

...never wished for anything...

Bayn had 'owned' the lamp before he gave it to Olivia. He'd never used the wish that would be his by right of ownership.

Could he still claim it?

What could he do with it?

How much power would it take to undo the spell? Undo the past?

He turned his attention to Gena, still enveloped by the protection of his essence, fear etched into her face.

She couldn't keep living this way.

Eat him. His dragon ordered.

We don't do that anymore.

Crunchy...

Bayn materialized his tail. It whipped out, striking Conrad and sending him flying upward several feet. It happened so fast Conrad didn't have time to react. He landed heavily, face down, and the lamp rolled free of his grasp.

Gena darted forward, snatching it away, and quickly backed into the safety of Bayn's cloud.

He wouldn't be able to hold this form forever. He needed to do something.

The sorcerer groaned, getting his wind back, struggling to his knees.

Bayn returned to his human form. "Gena, do you trust me?"

Startled, she said, "Yes."

"Give me the lamp."

She hesitated for only a second before shoving it into his hands.

He held the gleaming gold between his palms and concentrated on the right words.

"I have a wish owed to me by right of ownership," he said loud enough that Conrad would hear.

"No," he gasped.

Bayn turned to Gena, holding her gaze. Olivia had wished for Gena's freedom. Bayn needed to go a step further.

"I wish that *all* of Gena's power be hers alone to control."

"No!" Conrad shouted. "A djinn being returned to its power will be an uncontrollable force of destruction."

Bayn rolled his eyes.

Turning his full gaze back to Gena, he kissed her forehead. "I wish it." He whispered.

Flames appeared in her irises. She raised her fingers, where a larger flame appeared.

She snapped her fingers.

The lamp's golden glow increased, surging. A tether of gold reached out from it toward Gena, encircled her, and with a final flare, the lamp lost its unnatural luminescence.

She closed her eyes and sighed.

When she opened them again, the flames in her eyes flared and she smiled at Bayn.

She waved a hand toward Conrad, who turned to run for the rooftop door.

Freezing mid-stride, he was lifted from his feet and yanked backward. She drew her fist in toward herself, and Conrad followed.

He began to chant.

She frowned.

Her other hand raised, she pinched the air, causing Conrad's lips to pinch shut.

Bayn stepped back, waiting to see what she would do to the sorcerer.

Would she destroy him?

Hand held aloft, Conrad's body floated several feet from the gravel.

Gena turned her face to Bayn as though she waited for his reaction.

He gave her none.

What she did was her choice.

She walked up to Conrad. "I could blink you out of existence."

His eyes went wide, sliding toward Bayn, pleading.

"But that's too easy," she said, "You know—knew—my true name, at one time. But I am completely altered now, thanks to your spell. My essence has changed, that name is no longer who I am. You cannot use it against me again."

Gena's hands shook.

Conrad's mouth was still sealed shut.

"I take back the gift of longevity I bestowed upon you. That was my first mistake. No, that was my second mistake. The first was trusting you." She snapped her fingers. Gold mist rippled out from Conrad's form.

"My third mistake was to help you grow your magic. If I hadn't, you'd never have become powerful enough to trap me in the first place. I reclaim that knowledge. You will be reduced to the petty tricks you knew before I found you in the forest."

Conrad dropped in a heap.

"The only magic I will impose on you is the inability to exploit another soul. You will live out the remainder of your human life as you are."

The scream of sirens echoed in the distance, growing louder as it bounced off the concrete and glass buildings surrounding them.

Gena looked up at Bayn. "We should report the break in and destruction of your office window when the police arrive.

Bayn blinked, then smiled.

They both looked down at the lamp in his hands. He held it out to her.

"Why don't you hold on to it for a little while?"

He raised a brow.

She stood on tip toe and pressed her lips to his.

Chapter Eighteen

B ayn disconnected the call from his cell. "Kaylie says the phone's been ringing all morning. Patrons are signing subscriptions to support the museum. They're all eager to see the prized new acquisition—the ancient hand crafted lamp—exclusively on display at the new proposed museum."

Gena dropped the newspaper on the table. It slid a few inches toward Bayn.

The headline slashed the front page.

"Businessman Catches Intruder During High Profile Charity Gala Event, Attempting To Steal Priceless Lamp."

He looked up from his cereal bowl with a smirk. "If Conrad wasn't smart enough to estab-lish a solid human life with proper ID, I can't imagine how he's going to explain himself to the authorities."

Gena shrugged. "They can deal with him as they see fit. He's no longer my problem."

"Our problem," Bayn said.

She leveled her gaze on him as he finished the cereal and set the bowl aside.

"From the moment we found each other again, every problem became a shared problem. And will always be, so long as we're together."

Gena's heart flipped several times. Is that what you want? To be together?"

He nodded with a grin. "So long as you'll put up with me. If I were a wishing type, which I'm usually not, I'd wish for there to be an 'us' forever," He shrugged. "but that's up to you. I no longer take anything I want and just hoard it away. As much as I may want to."

"You want me?"

"I do."

Gena moved around the corner of the table. Bayn pulled her onto his lap.

Leaning down, she pressed her lips to his. "I want you, too. Forever."

He leaned back, looking up into her face. "Are you sure?"

She nodded. "My secret wish all those years ago was for this—a moment like this with you."

Bayn grinned up at her. "I've been waiting for you to say so since we met at Quinn's party."

She drew her thumb across his full lower lip. "I didn't feel I could say so, not with the way things were."

"I know." He kissed her thumb.

"I'm sure, if you are."

"I am."

"Okay," she said breathlessly, heart racing.

His hands encircled her hips, pulling her closer. She could feel his desire pressed to her. Her heart flipped, as it always did, when she became aware of him.

All other thoughts were distant as she stared at his lips, wanting them to be on her—all over her.

She loved those lips, so sensual, soft yet demanding. Unafraid to let her know what he wanted. But he didn't take from her. He gave her space to meet him.

It was time she let him know what she wanted. Him.

She wanted to claim him as her own.

As a dragon, he could have claimed her, as was his nature, she knew.

He hadn't. He wanted her to meet him. Be his equal.

And she would.

She raised her fingers. A flame appeared. He smiled, not looking at it.

Gena snapped her fingertips and they were now seated on the edge of Bayn's bed instead of the kitchen chair.

"Remember that dress you wore to Quinn's party?"

She raised a brow, smiled, and snapped her fingers again.

"That's the one." His hands slid up her waist. "I've been wanting to take it off you since I saw you in it."

Gena laughed.

His hands roamed every inch of her, making her shiver and gasp. By the time his fingers slid between her thighs, she ached for him.

He grinned, discovering she wasn't wearing panties.

Staring down at him, heavy lidded, her desire was crowding her brain. Her need for him.

She pushed him back, falling to the bed with him, lips locked with his. Her tongue swept his lip and he captured her mouth, taking over.

Her hands flitted over his pants, pushing at the band, reaching inside for him.

He filled her hand, hot and ready.

Her fingers closed around him, as his worked inside her.

They both groaned.

She climbed atop him.

Bayn's hands grasped her hips, sitting up.

Her arms encircled his wide shoulders.

"Mine," she whispered against the side of his neck just below his earlobe, as she sank down, taking him into her.

His fingers tightened, pushing her down onto him. She moaned.

Hands slid down her thighs, gently encouraging her to wrap her legs around his hips. She sank further and she thought she'd lose her mind.

He kissed the crook of her neck and echoed, "Mine."

Tilting his hips, she gasped as his tip struck her sweet spot.

Unable to stop herself, she moved her hips.

They ground against one another.

Seeking his lips, she claimed him as he drove into her.

She bounced down onto him, gasping and moaning until she came, fingers gripping his hair, head thrown back.

Leaning into her, he exploded, surging into her with a growl, forehead to her chest.

She rocked over him, riding the waves of their joint orgasm until reality slowly returned.

When she opened her eyes, she smiled. "Your eyes are glowing."

The corner of his mouth quirked, "So are yours."

She laughed.

He picked her up, and carried her to the mirror.

The sight of their reflection joined together was so erotic, she clenched around him.

He groaned. "If you keep that up, we won't make it to the office at all today."

"So?"

He chuckled, running a finger along her shoulder.

Turning her attention to its track, she saw a white marking in the shape of an elongated dragon, stretching from the crook of her neck to the tip of her shoulder.

Turning her gaze back to him, she saw a mark on his neck too, just below his ear.

A curling black flame with a pair of angled eyes peered back at her.

They'd marked each other.

Wrapping her legs tighter around his hips, she shifted her hips. "I think we should take the day off."

"Whatever you wish," he murmured, as he began to fill her again with a subtle growl.

Note to the Reader

Dear Reader,

Thank you so much for taking the time to read *Wish*. If you enjoyed it, please consider leaving a review on your favourite platform.

To get free downloads, join my newsletter and browse my library for more books, visit:

JodiKendrick.com

-Jodi

About Jodi Kendrick

Jodi Kendrick lives in Eastern Ontario Canada with her *Favourite Person* and chompy furbaby, while their adult children explore the wider world.

As a romance author, she writes in paranormal, fantasy, steampunk & gaslamp subgenres, and sometimes delves into urban fantasy and paranormal women's fiction. Her characters are often quirky, sometimes cranky, but they all woman-up and get the job done while their partners ensure they survive with all their bits and bobs attached.

A history enthusiast and word dabbler most of her life, she enjoys exploring 'beyond-the-everyday' and the 'time-before-now', discovering relationship threads weaving individuals through time and place. She's rarely seen without flashy notebooks and colourful pens.

Follow Jodi on Social Media:

Dragon Island

Dragon Heat

Enchanted Ardor

Wish

EveL Worlds : FUCN'A

Tough Nut
Diamond in the Ruff
Honeyed Nut
Gorilla in the Hiss
FUCN'A Collection One
Pedigree Collection

Finely Aged

Dragon Steel

Global Paranormal Security Agency

Awakened
Surfacing
Polestar
Aquatic Investigations
Prowler

The Kindred Chronicles

Healer
Mercenary

The Soaring Dragon Chronicles

Return Flight
Changeling